The Reality Game

and

The Little Black Box

A Nice Pair

Jesse S. Smith

Basementia Publications
Silverton, Oregon

The Reality Game and The Little Black Box
Jesse S. Smith

ISBN 978-0-9766423-2-9

Basementia Publications
Silverton, Oregon

Cover photo by Magda Ehlers via Pexels.

Fiction: Speculative / Psychological

Author's Preface

These stories are rooted in an earlier era.

It was a time when computer monitors were giant boxes filled with cathode ray tubes. It was a time when, if you wanted to buy an airplane ticket, you walked in to the office of a local travel agency, and they booked the ticket for you. It was a time when very few people had cell phones; and those few phones were just basic flip phones, with no GPS, and no apps. It was a time of the infancy of the Internet, when social media had not been invented, and people still read newspapers and books in their free time. It was a time of contemplation and inner quests.

Although begun earlier in Portland, I wrote the bulk of both these stories during the year I taught in Egypt, for the school year 2000-2001.

Neither was completely properly finished at that time; so I shelved them, but continued to occasionally revisit them both for many years afterwards.

The roots of these stories grew slow tendrils, which extended into newer times.

I wrapped up *The Little Black Box* in October of 2009; and finally brought *The Reality Game* to its present conclusion in late 2019. That's right: I wrote the first draft of this impressionistic short story over the course of some twenty years.

The protracted composition period accounts for some noticeable anachronisms. My advice to the reader is: Just go with it.

In overall tone, style, and subject matter, these two short darkly dreamlike novellas are a nice pair. Neither is quite long enough to be released as a full-length book in its own right; so I have elected to release them together.

I hope you will find them worthwhile.

~Jesse S. Smith
February 21, 2022

The Reality Game

Awakening

It doesn't matter who I am. I'm nobody special. I'm just some guy. I'm not so different from a lot of other guys out there.

When all this began, I was making an unspectacular wage at an uninteresting job that consumed most of my days. When I wasn't at work, I spent my time running blasé errands, eating junk food, and watching reruns on TV. My politics were mainstream; my religious views, noncommittal.

Before I met Destiny, my life was neither meaningful nor fulfilling, but at least I felt like I was more or less in control of it. I thought I knew what I was doing and what was going on around me.

I had no idea.

*   *   *

It all began when I awoke moderately late with a mild hangover in my uninteresting apartment, one nondescript Wednesday morning.

I had pressed snooze more times than I should have, and was probably going to be late for work, but I couldn't bring myself to care.

I stared at the wall, trying to adjust to consciousness. After a minute or two, I got up and peed, then stepped into the shower for a real quick soap off. To save time, I skipped shaving for the third day running, even though at three days my dark facial hair looks stubbly and unkempt.

I went downstairs and brewed some drip coffee with the flip of a switch. For breakfast I absentmindedly munched the same bowl of cereal I'd had every morning for the last three months at least.

I read a book while I was eating... and that's when I came alive.

Reading made my mind feel active, and at the same time allowed me to focus my attention on a time and place outside of the present. At the time, I was reading a fantasy novel, full of enchantments and dragons and mystical adventures through untamed realms of faerie beings. Immersing myself in this magical land allowed me to escape from my life. Thinking about being there helped me to forget that I am here. Focusing my attention outside of my physical reality was a habitually ingrained aspect of my daily life, an activity I engaged in from minute to minute without conscious thought. True boredom, in its purest form, is a luxury which is only available to those privileged enough to be unconcerned with the details of their immediate survival. Like everyone else I knew, I spent my life trying to escape from boredom.

I took my book with me and went out into the rain to catch the bus. I had already missed the bus I usually think of as "my" bus, and had to wait outside for a quarter of an hour, getting cold and wet, before the next bus arrived. The bus was crowded, and there were no seats available. I grabbed a handhold and pulled out my book, and for most of the journey I was marginally successful at shutting out the world around me, trading the bleak reality of a crowded city bus with a noisy engine for the exciting fantasy of a dark night in a magical haunted forest.

Reading is an excellent form of escapism.

Time and again, I have become engrossed in tales of pure fantasy: stories set in lands which are even less accessible to me than lands which are merely separated from me by a span of space, time, and the embellishment of the author. I felt more at home in Tolkein's Middle Earth, with its wizards and dragons and elves and goblins, than I felt in the supermarket downtown. I read *Alice in Wonderland* a number of times, imagining the splendor of having one's reality so frightfully twisted. In my imagination I have wandered the sands of the distant planet Arrakis-Dune with Paul Muad'Dib and the giant sandworms. And of course, as with so many of my age, I felt that the conquests and achievements of Luke Skywalker were equally my own.

At one time or another I have identified with many different protagonists. And yet my identification with each protagonist was always somehow imperfect. Even as I tried to lose myself in the imagined scenes, some mental objection always stood in the way and reminded me of the unreality and impossibility of the story, like a fly buzzing on a television screen.

I will never be a Prince of Arabia, or a tribal Chief. I have whiled away many an hour with legends of King Arthur; yet his is an era which has passed: it is no more accessible to me than the America of Lewis and Clark, or the Jerusalem of Jesus, or the island of the Swiss Family Robinson.

Romeo and Juliet is a most tragic tale; yet I have no desire to die tragically: I want to live triumphantly!

I am just not a Jack Kerouac kind of a guy. I can't see myself jumping trains or hitch-hiking or never knowing where my next meal is coming from or where I will be in the morning or whether I will find a place to sleep tonight. Part of me suggests that I should experiment with this lifestyle for a time, just for the experience; yet it is not an impulse I have followed.

Although I admire his independent attitude, I'm not a Hemingway kind of a character, either; because I hope to live a long life without ever serving any time in the military, and I don't fight bulls.

There is one famous fictional character with whom I may always identify: Holden Caulfield. However, he is the eternal adolescent, shocked and confused by the outrages perpetrated around him, unable to wrest control of his circumstances. He is an aspect of myself that I will never be able to purge, even if I wanted to spend my life savings on psychotherapy: not a role model who I want to intentionally emulate.

Thus engrossed in my book, I barely noticed when the bus reached my stop. I hastily replaced the book in my satchel and scrambled out the door of the bus, disembarking into a downpour, and hurried down the city sidewalk full of strangers towards the travel agency office where I worked.

I was lucky that when I got to work, the front desk receptionist was talking on the phone to a customer, so she couldn't say anything to me about my arrival time; and though I got a few dirty looks from my co-workers on the way to my desk, my boss was nowhere in sight.

Sighing with relief, I slipped in to my cubicle, and turned to my computer.

Endless Vistas

I flipped the switch from 0 to 1.

A motor whirred. A fan turned on. Some lights lit up. After a moment, there was a "beep."

I removed my wet jacket as I watched, and hung it over the back of my chair.

The screen of the huge CRT monitor blipped into life with a flash of white light, followed by words and numbers which meant nothing to me.

Some grinding noises preceded a series of clicks and whirs. Finally a picture emerged on the monitor: a tapestry of interlocking designs, the background of my basic operations platform.

My attention span was already challenged. I located a coffee cup that didn't seem to be growing any mold spores yet, and nonchalantly strolled out of my cubicle down the hall to the office coffee pot. This time I did pass my boss, but I just smiled and tried to look like I had been at work for at least half an hour already, even though my wet hair must have been a dead giveaway. Once again I was lucky: she was deep in conversation with an accountant, and didn't even look at me.

Back in my cubicle, I entered a password to log on to the network, and another password that allowed me to access the client database. Most of my day would be spent referencing and updating that damn database. It was a far cry from rescuing a princess in distress, but it paid the rent.

I surveyed my domain. My desktop was cluttered with the disorganized paraphernalia of my lifestyle. The jetsam from a paper tsunami was strewn across my desktop: a jumble of letters, forms, documents, advertisements, memos from other people, and memos from my responsible side to the me that hides away here: scattered, stacked, and push-pinned to the removable walls of my cubicle next to postcards of holiday beaches from relatives, satisfied customers, and friends who I never see but e-mail occasionally. The piles of papers were obscured by empty wrappers from the processed carbohydrates and refined sugars I frequently bought out of the vending machine. All around the perimeter of this mess, and placed haphazardly on top of the papers, were empty coffee mugs in various states of uncleanliness, all stained brown with the residue of my favorite chemical stimulant. If I were a different sort of person, I might have cleaned up the wrappers and cups; but I am not that sort of person, so I ignored them. Instead, I tried to find a pen. My desk is a black hole for pens; they disappear and are never seen again. After a moment, I finally located an old ballpoint that was almost out of ink. I didn't have time to find another, though, for at that moment, the phone rang. I had sort of unrealistically hoped the phone would not ring all day, or at least not until after the coffee had scrubbed away my hangover, but I was not so lucky. There would be no break in the routine for me.

"Horizons Unlimited, Ltd., Tim speaking," I growled into the mouthpiece.

The caller was one of these people who basically want to read you the whole damn website. It was boring, but at least the conversation didn't require much participation from me. I could just say, "uh huh" or "that's right," every once in a while, and otherwise let my mind wander away.

As my caller talked, my gaze drifted across the lake of disorganized papers that had flooded my desktop, and up the wall to the papers I had push-pinned to the removable walls of my cubicle, interspersed with my tropical paradise beaches calendar and my collection of exotic postcards: glossy rectangles with bright, almost garish pictures of wide green landscapes, castles, and holiday beaches.

Everybody loves a holiday. That's why I had a job at a travel agency.

As my caller spoke, I had absentmindedly written something on a piece of paper with the ineffective ballpoint, and was going over and over the letters to darken them. I hadn't really thought about it much as I was writing it, I just put the letters down, one after another.

"There are many lands in which I rule," it read. I gulped some more coffee, opened another browser window, and typed in an address.

This was the personal side project which I hoped would answer the perplexing question of how to find the perfect trap door: an exit out of my daily life of discontent, and down the rabbit hole into a totally unexpected Wonderland.

I was creating another world. It was a sort of novel, but it was also an interactive role-playing game; or at least, that's what I wanted it to be, eventually. I dreamed that parts of it would be someday produced in a 3-D multi-player video game format.

I imagined a computer program encompassing such a bewildering variety of variables that it could actually respond to each individual user by creating completely unique scenarios in personally tailored realities: scenarios that responded realistically and unpredictably to the user's every action. I imagined all this displayed in a room that could project realistic holographs from all its walls, creating people and scenery to interact with the user.

Unfortunately, I lacked the budget, the knowledge, and the connections to make it happen. Also, the technology doesn't exist yet. In the absence of this technology, I figured my idea, if I ever got it completed, would end up being portrayed in flat, pixelated images with unrealistic movements. I mean, sure, modern interactive multi-player video games have pretty good graphics; but you'd never mistake them for something that was actually happening around you.

The finished product wasn't as interesting to me as the actual process of creating the world. I told myself that I put the time in because someday it might be worth something; but in truth, I invested my time because this was how I wanted to be spending my time, right now.

I posted all my ideas on my blog (under a pseudonym, of course). My friend Paul had helped me set up the website. We called the "e-scape." The homepage had a description of our project's eventual goal, and links to past and current installments of our ongoing storyline.

I found that this process of creation was a better form of escapism than anything else I could do to duck away from my surroundings during a typical workday.

Yes, for although due to larger societal influences and forces beyond my control I may sometimes lack a certain amount of direct authority over my most immediately tangible reality, in my imagination I had supreme godlike powers: I could create and destroy worlds, I could alter the destinies of entire civilizations. My bland daily experience was just something I had to get through in order to reach the true purpose of my life: like a layer of dirt and mud caked around a precious gemstone.

My job was just something I did to pay the bills; I never thought of it as what I was actually DOING with my life. It was merely a task that had to be completed (or sometimes, dodged) to allow me the leeway to pursue the secret hobby that really gave me a true sense of purpose.

I enjoyed getting caught up in this creative process. I liked to imagine all the possibilities, and felt a sort of power in choosing which of those possibilities would come to life, and then creating the details that would bring a vague and hazy potential into a clearly focused existence.

At times, when I was feeling inspired, creating this alternate reality was even more engaging than watching television or movies.

I would work on it in my free time, from the comfort and privacy of my own home, late into the night.

The posts on the blog had evolved into a sort of continuing story with a more or less coherent plotline. The setting jumped around a lot; sometimes the story took place in outer space, sometimes in medieval fields, sometimes within the borders of the Kingdom of Faerie itself; and often it was set in the crowded, technology obsessed world of the present day or the near future. Only occasionally did our hero venture into a sort of post-nuclear holocaust world, but yes, he went there, too. Wherever the story took place, the hero always found himself in the midst of inexplicable circumstances which he must understand in order to avert a disastrous situation, and he was always nearly out of time in which to accomplish this. Maybe it was derivative in some of its inspiration. I didn't care. I'd gotten so hooked on the habit of creating this world, for myself and my friends, that I maintained the site and posted new installments for the storyline with an almost religious sort of manic obsession.

I had not been listening. Lost in my thoughts about the next installment of our continuing storyline, I didn't notice at first that my caller had asked me a question. Suddenly the silence on the other end of the line alerted me that she was waiting for some kind of response.

I just was not with it that day. It took me three tries before I could properly start the sentence to answer her. The words were there, somewhere in my brain; and my mouth was moving, somewhere else, but some essential connection between the two seemed to be missing.

"Well, but, yes, I mean, obviously, our goal here at Horizons Unlimited, Ltd. is to ensure that all of our customers are not merely satisfied by their experience with us, but are so overjoyed that they will tell all their friends and give us some free advertising!" I blabbered thoughtlessly.

Jesus, why did I say that? Nobody wants to hear themselves described as "free advertising."

There was a silence on the other end of the line for a moment.

During that moment, part of my mind irrelevantly mentioned that it wanted to have sex, while another part of my mind instructed my mouth to launch into one of my memorized shpiels about payment plans and frequent customer bonuses.

"So, uh," I blundered on, "of course we guarantee that if you pay for something that's, um, nice, then," was I really saying this? "you'll have a really, nice, experience with it," I trailed off. Get back on message. "Would you like to place an order? Or I could send you a color brochure, if you'd like---"

"No, I don't think so, not right now," she interrupted me. "This is all very expensive."

"Well, we do have some economy packages, too, currently, if you're interested in," I began tentatively, but I was already anticipating her next words.

"I'll have to think about it," she said. "Thanks for your time."

"Thanks for calling Horizons Unlimited, Ltd.," I said, but before I even got the words out, I was already listening to a dial tone.

Muttering to myself, I minimized my web browser and pulled up the customer database.

My routine at work was divided between the telephone and my computer. When the phone wasn't ringing, I spent my time looking up customer accounts, entering orders, processing payments, and replying to e-mails. I even helped with publicity mailings sometimes, but usually I was kept too busy answering the phone.

My talents are, of course, more than adequate to all of these tasks; and yet, at times I would find myself behaving in a shy and insecure manner around my co-workers. I suspected that they didn't like me, although nobody had ever said anything specifically derogatory to me. I felt distanced from them. I imagined that they disliked me because I was one of the youngest people at the office; or because I was a man in his mid-twenties with the facial hair of a stereotypical sociopath; or maybe because I read fantasy novels; or perhaps due to my lack of interest in football; or possibly because I was not an avid Christian; or simply because they suspected me of drinking alcohol or using drugs, or of hanging out with unsavory friends, or of showing up late to work and slacking off and shirking responsibility throughout the day. I don't know where people get these kinds of crazy ideas. But it doesn't really matter, because in my own mind I am the greatest bad-ass who has ever lived.

There was a big stack of paper forms sitting there, and it was my job to enter them into the database, and then file them. I was just getting to it when the phone rang again. I muttered a swear word or two, then picked up the phone and tried to sound overjoyed as I said, "Horizons Unlimited, Ltd., Tim speaking."

"Hello, Tim," said my caller. It sounded like it might be the same lady with whom I had just been speaking.

"Good morning," I said, trying to sound exceptionally glad to hear from her while I wondered why she had called me back. But the next moment, I was no longer so sure it was the same person, because her next words were a complete non sequitur.

"Are you happy with your life?" she asked me.

"Excuse me?" I asked in surprise.

"Your life," she said. "The one you're living. The way you spend your time every day. Does it make you happy?"

"Uh," I said, "yeah, I'm fine, thanks. How are you?" I hoped that my colleague shuffling papers in the next cubicle, who could certainly overhear this conversation, would assume the caller had asked me if I was having a nice day or something.

"Do you feel fulfilled by your work?" she pressed. "Do you find that the things you work on are important and meaningful to you?"

"I'm sorry, what?" I said, to avoid her question. At this point I figured she was probably making phone calls for Jesus, and I was looking for a polite way of hanging up on her.

"Does every moment bring you a new revelation of the splendors of life and the interrelationships of all things? Does your job really mean something to you?"

"Well, I, uh, don't know about revelations," I admitted, "it's still kind of early in the morning; but I can tell you what my job means to me: it means the rent gets paid."

"Huh," she said, sounding incredibly unimpressed. I was about to make some attempt to steer our conversation back to something business related when she continued. "What would you say is the purpose of your work?"

"Oh, well," I said with some relief, since this question almost seemed relevant, "I help people make travel arrangements.

"Mostly," I explained, "I obtain plane tickets for couples who are going on vacation. I mean, actually I do a lot of scheduling for business trips, too; but even business trips are a break in the routine. They send me postcards, sometimes, while they're off on their voyages, visiting beaches, resorts, and tourist attractions in the far corners of the world. They send me pictures of the landscapes, the mountains, the golf courses, the theme park characters, and the street signs of the places they visited in their destinations foreign and domestic on their quests for enlightenment, entertainment, financial success, or a simple break in the monotony of their daily humdrum existence. Everybody loves a holiday," I concluded brightly. "I sell holidays. People dream of holidays. So really what I do is, I sell dreams."

"I'm sure," she said, sounding dubious and not at all sure. "But do you appreciate a holiday less if you don't have a daily life to go back to?"

"I'm sorry?" I asked. I had no idea what she was talking about. The question seemed rhetorical, and not really directed to me.

"If you could change everything, radically," she asked, "just abandon everything and be someone else, somewhere else, would you do it?"

"I don't know," I answered truthfully. "I mean, if I abandoned my life and started over, I'd lose the title to my car, because technically the bank owns it right now."

"You work for Horizons Unlimited, Ltd., right?"

"Yes, that's who you called, ma'am," wondering what kind of a nut job I had on the line here.

"How is that working for you?" she asked, speaking rapidly. "Are your own personal horizons really, truly unlimited?

"Uh, yeah," I lied, "I would have to say so."

"So," she said flatly, "what you're saying is, you are so content with your life that you wouldn't be willing to risk what you have for an opportunity to do something different."

"Why are you asking me this?" I finally worked up the courage to ask.

"I'm just wondering, is all," she lied.

"Do you always have conversations like this with telephone salesmen?" I asked.

"I don't usually talk to a lot of telephone salesmen," she told me.

I tried to think of what I should say next.

I was intrigued by her unusual questions; this conversation was certainly an atypical break in the routine. At the same time, I was somewhat annoyed, because I had work to do, and this philosophical conversation with someone who didn't seem to be planning to buy anything was a waste of my time. In the end, I decided that my function as a Customer Service Representative was to make every caller feel that Horizons Unlimited,

Ltd. was deeply interested in every client's personal concerns. Keeping the callers happy was my job, whether they made a purchase a not. I could keep this strange caller happy by answering a couple of simple, if somewhat personal, questions. I was just about to say something along those lines when she spoke first, seeming to anticipate my line of thought.

"I'm sorry," said my caller, who still had not introduced herself. "I know you're busy with your work, and I'm not trying to pry into your personal life. I'm just..."

She paused, and it was my turn to interrupt her before she had a chance to finish.

"No, it's okay," I said. "I'm not trying to be a tight-ass. I'm just, I guess I have to admit that callers don't usually ask me those kinds of questions."

I tried to remember what the question was. The caffeine had helped, but my brain still felt like a slug: slow-moving, brown, and oozing slime.

"I think," I said slowly, "that the reason I don't drop everything to do something else on a daily basis is that, well, I'd have to be pretty convinced that the alternative would be better than the status quo. You know? The people I've known who do act on those kinds of impulses regularly, tend to have trouble with things like steady employment and day to day cash flow." Finally, I thought of a way to bring the conversation back around to business. "Which is why tourism is such a popular vacation idea. You can go somewhere else, and live a different life, for a while, with the reassurance that at the end of the vacation, you'll be able to return home to the life that is familiar to you."

"But would you still appreciate a holiday if you didn't have a daily life to go back to?" she murmured. I almost wasn't sure what she had said. Hadn't she already said that before? Was she repeating herself now? The conversation seemed to be going in circles. Perhaps question was directed more to herself than to me. I was confused.

I tried to respond in my most jocular fashion; because whatever this lady's problem was, I didn't want her to tell me about it right now. "Well, uh, actually, you know," I said, sounding very intelligent, "a lot of folks go to places like the Caribbean, and they like it so much that they just settle down there, and they never come back!"

She chuckled. "You're a good salesman... What did you say your name was?"

"Tim," I told her. "My name's Tim O'Brien. Anytime you call Horizons Unlimited, Ltd., just ask for me, and I'd be happy to help you with anything that you – "

"Actually," she interrupted my commission spiel, "I was wondering if you might tell me something."

"Sure," I said, preparing to launch into a prepared presentation of our special offers and maybe clinch a sale out of this lengthy phone call after all, "we have a great package deal for--"

But she cut me off again. "I was hoping," she said, "that you could discuss it with me in person."

"In person?" I said. "Oh, well, uh, do you know where our office is? It's--"

"Yes, I know where your office is," she cut me off. "I actually work just down the street."

"Oh, great, well you can just swing by, and anybody who's available can..."

"I don't want to talk to whoever is available, Tim. I want to talk to *you*. You've been very helpful."

"Oh, uh, okay," I said, feeling embarrassed. "Well, when would you like to come by?"

"What are you doing for lunch today, Tim?"

"I don't know," I said truthfully. On slow days I could sometimes leave the office long enough to grab some take-out from the Thai food restaurant across the street. More often, I was lucky if I had enough break time to take a piss, and I would eat a late lunch of junk food and snack food, on the fly, at my desk, shoveling calories into my mouth without noticing what it was or what it tasted like because I was so involved in catching up on one project or another in between the incessant ringing of the telephone.

"I think you should have lunch with me," my caller told me.

"Lunch?" I said. I really had not been expecting this. It seemed a little bit creepy. I really just wanted to limit our contact to the phone

In my imagination, I pictured her as a neurotic, middle-aged, personally repellent individual, and I would prefer playing computer solitaire to being obliged to talk business with her during my precious break time; but she didn't give me a chance to say so.

"How's the Tom Kha Kung?" she asked me.

"The what?"

"You know," she breathed in erotic tones, "the Thai food place across the street from your office. Mmmm," she almost moaned in my ear. "I always see it when I drive past, but I've never been in."

"Oh, uh, yeah, it's pretty good," I admitted.

"All right, I'll see you there at about one o'clock, then, okay?" she went on in a brusquely businesslike voice, and I wondered if she and I were both having the same conversation.

"Well, I can, uh, I mean I'll have to ask my..."

"Great. See you then. Gotta go. Bye."

"But who--" I started to say, but the line clicked, and a dial tone buzzed in my ear.

"That was weird," I thought. I looked at the handset as if it could answer the questions mosquito-ing around in my head, such as, who the heck am I supposed to be meeting at lunch today?

My musings were soon interrupted by yet another phone call.

Destiny

While the next caller read the website to me, I got a new e-mail notification. It was my old friend Paul. By now it's been so long, I don't even remember what he was writing about that morning. It was some nonsense about the e-scape blog, I think. Hearing from Paul prompted a lengthy flashback in my mind, and I recalled a conversation that he and I had once had about reality-warping microchip brain implants; but in the great story of my life, that particular digression did not immediately move the plot forward.

As it happened, all my co-workers slipped out for lunch at the same time that all the other people from all over the state were calling in to our office on THEIR lunch breaks. With nobody else to grab the lines, I was hard put just to pick up all the calls, take a number, and promise that somebody would call back.

I fielded call after call. My co-workers started to trickle back in to the office, but by then I had a whole list of calls to return, and a pile of partially completed forms, and an exponentially multiplying population of Post-It notes all over my cubicle. I was going crazy from the coffee in my brain and the coffee that wanted out of my bladder.

I was so wrapped up in my work that I almost forgot I was supposed to meet some anonymous potential customer for lunch.

At about one o'clock I started to feel like I was forgetting something, but dismissed it because nothing more specific came to mind and there were so many things I had to get done in the shortest time possible.

I shook my head. I looked at the little clock on my computer screen. Then finally I realized that one of my little yellow sticky notes read, "1 PM Lunch." It was already ten after!

The phone rang. I looked at it; then I decided to ignore it. I bolted for the bathroom, then threw on my jacket. I passed my boss on the way out the door, said, "Lunch appointment, potential customer, be back," and didn't wait for her approval or for any response at all.

I think she started to say, "Oh, Tim, before you go, would you," but I surprised myself when I didn't even let her finish.

I just said, "Already late," and left the office at a run.

I managed to narrowly avoid getting hit by a car as I crossed the street, then entered the Thai food restaurant, feeling foolish. I had no idea who I was supposed to be meeting; she had told me neither her name nor what she looked like.

Inside the door, with the babble of voices over the piped in light ethnic music, I stood in a line, looking at the statues of dragons, and the prints of nature paintings by Buddhist monks. I looked around at the people at the tables. There were several groups of four or more, laughing and talking; there were one or two couples out for a romantic meal; but at first I couldn't see anybody who looked like they were there waiting to meet me.

Finally, just as the hostess was approaching me, I saw a woman sitting by herself at a small table in the corner; but I automatically discounted the possibility that this woman could possibly be the person waiting for me, for one very simple reason: she was far too good-looking. I resumed my scan for a neurotic middle-aged woman, but didn't see any who were sitting alone.

The hostess asked me if I was by myself, and I told her I was supposed to meet somebody.

"So, table for two, sir?" she asked in her heavily accented English.

"Well, I kind of thought she might be here already," I mumbled, looking around hopelessly.

"You Team?" the hostess said.

"What?"

"You Team?" she repeated.

"Oh, yeah, I'm Tim," I said with a smile.

"This way, sir," she said. The hostess led me straight to the table in the corner where the slim young woman I had seen before was sitting alone. She had mouse-brown hair and nice clothes, and she sipped a cup of tea as she read a thick book. She looked up from it as we approached, and I got an impression of her pretty face: little or no makeup, tastefully dangly earrings, and wide, bright eyes.

"Hi," I said, feeling very awkward all of a sudden, "I'm Tim O'Brien from Horizons Unlimited, Ltd. I don't know if it was you I was talking to on the---"

"Hi, Tim," she interrupted me, and smiled. "My name is Destiny. Pull up a chair."

We shook hands, and I sat down. "Nice to meet you, Destiny," I said.

"Likewise," she replied.

I looked at the menu, then remembered I owed her an apology.

"I'm sorry I'm late," I began, "it's really busy at the..."

"Not to worry, I only got here a very few short minutes ago, and I've barely had time to open my book. It was nice to relax. I'm sorry your work is so stressful."

Just then the waitress came over, and poured me some tea. I already knew what I wanted, because one of those Thai menu items that I'd enjoyed before was just calling my name, so we placed our orders.

After the waitress left, I looked over at Destiny, who was watching me expectantly. I was having trouble moving my attention past her appearance, which was quite striking. My eyes lingered on her nicely full lips, and tried not to think about how perfectly they complemented the curve of her breasts. It was going to be difficult for me to think about travel package prices and special combination offers while sitting across the table from this woman.

I tried to make some light conversation. "Thanks for inviting me out to lunch," I said. "I'm glad to have an excuse to get away from the office when it's crazy and hectic like that." Not what I was supposed to say. I looked down at my hands, then back at Destiny, who was still looking at me expectantly, as if she was waiting for me to do something.

I didn't know what else to do, so I turned my mind to business and asked, "So, did you want to plan a vacation?" She probably just wanted me to tell her about package deals to tropical resorts, I thought. I should have brought some flyers with me.

"I am interested," Destiny replied vaguely, "in a change of scenery."

"Well, you could go to Greece," I suggested. "Some of the world's finest beaches are there on the Mediterranean, plus you'd have the opportunity to see Athens, the Parthenon, the Acropolis, plenty of old world relics with all the conveniences of – "

"How many different kinds of travel does your firm specialize in?" she interrupted.

"Uh, well we do have an affiliate relationship with some cruise lines, but we're mostly focused on air travel," I explained. "And we sometimes procure Eurail passes for people, but generally, most folks like to get their own train or bus tickets once they've arrived at their destination country; and of course, it's impossible for us to guarantee any kind of accuracy in the public transit schedule, from all the way over here in America."

"Tim," she said abruptly, "do you ever wonder what you're doing with your life?"

I didn't answer at once.

She was looking at me intently.

Finally I said slowly, "Look, I don't mean to be rude, or anything, but why exactly did you want to meet me here? Because if you aren't interested in, you know, business, or anything, just say so, and I won't hassle you with business, and we can just discuss Chinese philosophy for a while, or whatever floats your boat. It's just that, I'm not sure I get it. What exactly did you call me for?"

She let the silence build ominously before she replied. Finally she said, "Do you remember what I said to you on the phone this morning?"

I thought about this for a few seconds, then said, "Yeah, you, uh, you asked me if I get mystical revelations from my job, and then you asked if I would abandon my life to do something different."

"Have you thought about that at all?"

"I have to be perfectly honest with you, Destiny, I really haven't had time to think about much of anything at all today. It's been really busy at work."

"Do you enjoy that?"

"Well, sometimes it's kind of stressful, but generally I prefer being active to being bored."

"Do you often get bored at work?"

"Not usually," I said, then chuckled as I recalled my earlier train of thought. "Boredom is a luxury for the privileged." She looked at me with an inscrutably blank expression. "Uh, anyways," I went on, running my mouth to fill the silence, "there's always paperwork to do, coffee to drink, co-workers to talk to, e-mails to write; you know," I ended lamely, "I keep busy.'"

"Is this what you see yourself doing for the rest of your life?" she asked.

"What, working as a travel agent?" I asked in surprise. "Probably not, no," I admitted, "but I, uh–"

"I mean keeping busy," she clarified. "Will you spend the rest of your life just keeping busy?"

Once again, her line of questioning was deviating far from holiday hot spots. I wrote off all hope of selling her tickets, and decided to see if I could get her into bed instead.

"Well, yeah," I said, "I hope I'll always be doing things. I like to think of myself as an active person, you know? I take long walks, I read books, I think about the nature of reality, and stuff."

"And what," she asked with renewed interest, "do you think about the nature of reality?"

"I can't predict it," I admitted. "I don't always know what's going to happen next." Why was she asking me all these questions? I felt like I was being interrogated, and I still didn't know anything about her.

Jesse S. Smith

"The nature of reality is a subject of great interest to me, too," she told me.

"And what do *you* think about reality?" I asked, glad to finally be the one asking a question for a change.

"Well," she said contemplatively, "personally, I believe in free will and random chance; but sometimes I have to wonder if that's the whole story."

She looked down, staring pensively at the astrological placemat, which told you what kind of person you are and who you should marry based on what year you were born in.

I blurted out the question that had been bothering me. "So why a travel agent?"

She looked up at me and laughed. The waitress brought out our Spring Roll appetizers. Destiny contemplated hers before delicately nibbling at it. I dipped mine in hot sauce and bit into it hungrily, realizing that I hadn't eaten anything in hours. We chewed in silence. I wondered if my companion would ever divulge any information about herself. Probably not, I thought. I'd get back to the office with nothing to show for my "business lunch," no tickets sold, no phone number or personal history from my prospect. I determined not to let my boss make me feel guilty about my sudden and unfruitful departure – she owed me break time, dammit...

"You seem like a guy who would be interested in going places," Destiny answered at last, interrupting my reverie.

"Myself personally?" I laughed. "I wish I had the time and money to visit just a fraction of the places I sell tickets to."

"Tim," she said, "your body doesn't have to move for you to go places. Travel is a state of mind. It's about experiencing what you're seeing as something new, being intrigued by your surroundings, thinking about unusual things, maybe learning new languages. When you travel you have to acquaint yourself with unfamiliar systems, train times, airports, customs officials. Traveling makes your brain work.

"Lots of travel is also a vacation; and while on vacation, people use their free time to relax. You might read a magazine on the airplane, go out to clubs and get drunk, have an affair, watch a movie: everybody has their own favorite pastime.

"The trick," she continued, "is to understand that you don't have to go to South America to learn Spanish, and you don't have to go to India to have a religious experience; just like you don't have to go to Amsterdam to smoke marijuana, and you don't have to go to Thailand to have sex with a prostitute who used to be a man. You can direct your own experiences very deliberately. You can decide to make your life the way you want it to be."

"I feel like you're getting at something here," I said, "but I'm not sure what."

"Tim," she said, "what is your purpose in life?"

"What?" I asked. I was by now completely convinced that my attractive lunch companion had ingested a massive dose of psychoactive psychotropic pharmaceuticals before coming here to meet me. I tried to notice if there was anything strange about the dilation of her pupils. And I tried to answer the question. "Well, in a strictly Darwinian sense, my purpose is to survive long enough to reproduce and preferably to ensure the survival of my progeny, thereby doing my part to assist the continuation of the species."

"Come on, Tim, I'm talking about your personal goals. Your life is more than working to pay the rent. What do you hope to achieve eventually? Behind the front that you must maintain for your basic everyday social interactions, what are you trying to accomplish eventually?"

"I don't know, Destiny," I said truthfully. "I've always been a bit of a nihilist. I'm not convinced that *anything* I can do will ever achieve a useful or productive goal. But why am I the one answering all the personal questions here?" I demanded. "I still don't know who you are, what you do, or why you asked me out to lunch. I have the feeling that you're not interested in a package deal from my travel agency."

"Everything is a package deal, Tim, and those questions of yours mean nothing. I could give you any kind of true or false answer to any of them, and where would it get you? Would you begin to develop a sense of trust in me through feeling that you know me better? Don't do it, Tim. Anything I tell you about myself will be just a story, even if it's mostly true."

"I don't understand," I said.

"What's there to understand?" she replied. "Anything that anybody tells you at any time is going to be warped by their own subjective interpretation. The reality of any situation is only that which can be perceived by your senses, and even they can be tricked to a certain extent. How can you ever know what's really real?"

"It's never given me too much trouble," I maintained sulkily.

"But imagine," she said contemplatively, "how interesting your life would be, if you were a little less certain."

"Sounds kind of scary."

"Haven't you ever found fear exciting?"

"Sure, but movies and carnival rides are a controlled environment," I disagreed.

"Well," she hesitated, "maybe you're not ready."

"Ready for what?"

"Well, if you're not ready for it, then I can't tell you."

"Okay," I said. "Let's say, just for argument's sake, that I've just been pretending that I'm not ready, so I can distort your perception of reality."

Destiny favored me with a smile. "That's very good," she said. "If that's the case, then you are ready indeed."

"Ready for what?" I asked again.

"Ready for instructions."

"Instructions?" I repeated, carried away by my role-playing. "What is this, the Green Berets? The Navy SEALS? I never joined no military, and I don't take orders from anybody."

"Not orders," she said. "Instructions, like how to play a game. The instructions are just a framework of guidelines. Nobody can tell you what moves to make; the course of the game is up to you. It's only the format and structure that others can tell you, and this game is very loosely structured." She looked at me with an expression I could not interpret. "You," she said, "have probably already been playing without even knowing it."

"All right," I said, "I'm hooked. What is it?"

"Have you ever tried to leave behind the reality of your daily routine and the dull grey bleakness of life, to escape into a reality of your own construction where you are totally in control, endowed with the ability to do great things – even if this alternate reality only exists inside your own mind?"

"Of course," I said, "all the time."

"We have found a way to blur the distinction," she said, "between that world and this one."

"Who's 'we'?"

"The ones who play the game."

"What game?"

"We just call it the Reality Game, for lack of a better name; but really, it's much more than simple escapism."

"Are we talking about a computer game, or a board game, or what?"

"No, that's the beauty of it. There's nothing artificial: no game tokens, no specific place you have to go... This is a way of life you can take with you. You can play it wherever you are, just by doing the things you do."

"And this is different from my daily life because?"

"I'm talking about an improvisational street theater," she said. "Everyone around you is an actor, although they may not be aware of it; and you are the script's co-writer. When life starts to get too boring and predictable for the characters of the moment, you liven things up a bit by making something completely unexpected happen." After a pause, at last she concluded, "I only want to be certain that you're the kind of person we're looking for."

"*Who* is looking for *what*?" I said, completely conflusterated.

"Oh, we're all looking for something," she said with assurance, "it's just that some of us aren't sure what it is."

"True enough," I said, wishing she would change the subject or be more specific or something, because this style of interaction was really starting to get to me.

"We've been interested in you for a long time now," said Destiny.

"Once again," I demanded, "who's 'we?' And why are you interested in me?"

"We call ourselves the Game Masters, and we have been reading your online journal," she told me, and didn't offer any more immediate explanation.

I tried not to react. "What online journal is that?" I said.

She just looked at me, one eyebrow cocked ever so slightly.

I tried to say nothing.

She was rummaging through her handbag. After a moment, she produced a manila envelope marked with my name, from which she extracted a whole sheaf of papers. There were documents covered in text; photographs of me taken in a number of places, always at times when I clearly didn't know I was being photographed; and a high-resolution full-color printout of the homepage of our e-scapism website. Attached to this was a thick sheaf of paper consisting, I discovered, of all the writings I'd posted there over the course of the past several years. As I had lost some of the originals, Destiny in fact possessed a more extensive collection of my recent works than I did myself. Her collection of my writings dated back all the way to the website's debut. I was astonished, and scared.

"What is all this?" I demanded.

"It's just our file on you," she said, dismissively indicating the dossier with a sweep of her hand. "We have a lot of connections. We know things, and we cultivate relationships with people who know things. We've been monitoring your activities, working up a profile on you to determine what sort of role you would play, so to speak, as a member of our organization."

I decided to try to deny it. "I have no idea what any of that is," I lied badly. "It has nothing to do with me."

With a slight half-smile, she sorted through the sheaf, and retrieved a printout of my friend's social networking page, where he named me as the author of the blog. His post included a link to my own social networking page, on which was listed my place of employment, and a photograph of myself. "It's okay, Tim, you don't have to lie. We know who you are, and we want you to play our game; but we want you to play of your own free will." She raised an eyebrow. "Not everyone is given the choice."

I started to feel suspicious and perhaps even slightly paranoid.

"Do you work for the government?" I asked.

"No, Tim," she said, "our organization has no political or religious affiliations. We like to think of our true purpose as a form of enlightening entertainment."

"So, you're telling me that you work for, like, the Zen branch of a Hollywood movie studio, or something?"

"It's more subtle than that. We don't produce anything; we don't make movies or CD's or any kind of profit. The entertainment we seek and produce is so refined, it exists solely for the purity of itself and the revelations it enables us to attain."

"I'm sorry, Destiny," I finally managed to say, "but it sounds like a scam. In my experience, there are no individual selves whose motivations are so pure as the ones you just described."

"We play the Reality Game for fun. Don't you ever do anything just for fun?" Something about the way she sat as she said it projected a wave of sexuality that washed over me and left me soaked by a confused state of desire.

"That's not a real question," I argued, fighting the distraction of my hormonal urges. "It's only rhetorical. What if I said no? No, Destiny, I never do anything just for fun."

"Tim," she said at last, "we're very interested in the untapped potential of creative minds like yours. Someone like you who can dream up all kinds of new realities is someone who would be ideally suited to join our Reality Game and create interesting twists in the collective reality we all share."

It started to rain outside. I watched out the window as people on the street covered their heads with their jackets and ran for shelter. I wasn't at all sure that I wanted to get involved in Destiny's game; but she was very beautiful, and by now I was very curious.

"And how is it," I asked, "that you twist reality?"

"That," she said, "is what we want you to help us imagine. What would you do, if you could do something to make people really question everything about their lives?"

"Uh," I said, totally unsure of what I should say, "well, I guess people would really think about their lifestyles if they had to live without electricity for a day."

"That's true," she said, in a disappointed voice that clearly communicated that I was not living up to the mark, "but maybe start by thinking small, working on an individual level; and remember that although we might sympathize with your sentiments, we are not by nature a political organization."

"What would I do," I said slowly, "to twist the reality of an individual," she nodded, "in a totally bizarre yet life-affirming manner?" A smile. "Shit, Destiny, I think you did it to me. I mean, you pop up from out of nowhere and you know all this shit about me and you have fucking photographs of me, like your people have been following me around or something, and you offer me a position in this mysterious organization of yours: you're freaking me out, it would freak anybody out to suddenly have a stranger know all about you."

"Keep going with that," she encouraged, "but try to imagine a scenario that's different from your own. We don't usually learn so much about the people we play our game with."

"And, you say, they don't always know that they're playing your game?"

"True," she said primly. "As I said, not everyone is given the choice."

"So you could maybe just learn a little bit about somebody, like their name and maybe where they tend to go at certain times, and have random strangers approach them and call them by name."

"Tell me more about that."

"Okay, so there's this guy, right? Let's say his name is Bob. Bob takes the bus to work every day, and one morning, just as he's about to get on the bus, a passenger who is getting off waves at him and says, 'Hi, Bob,' and Bob looks, only it's not someone Bob has ever met before, maybe not even the kind of person Bob would normally associate with." Destiny's eyes sparkled, but she said nothing. "So Bob thinks to himself, well that's weird, but doesn't give it much more thought, until at lunch that day he goes to his favorite bagelry or whatever, and just as he's entering through the door, someone says, 'Hi, there, Bob, it's great to see you,' and walks out before Bob can ask any questions. Bob is perplexed as to how this person knew his name, but has no choice other than to keep going about his day. As he's leaving the shop, some kid walks up to him and says, 'Yo, Bob, wassup,' and walks off. Maybe Bob follows this kid and says, 'Hey, how did you know my name?' but the kid just shrugs and says, 'Some dude came up to me and asked me to say hi to you when you came out of the store.'"

Contemplating this, I was debating what direction to take my scenario in, how I could add richness or maybe take it a step further, but Destiny interrupted my thoughts.

"That's excellent, Tim," she complimented me, "truly amazing. You just described a variation of one of our favorite pranks! Now we've reached a point where we're trying to supersede all that, go beyond anything we've ever done before, and take our Reality Game to the next level.

"Think about it for a while. How can you really shake the foundations of everything that someone has tried so hard for years and years to not ask questions about? How can you make the commonplace seem uncommon, and thereby prime unwitting students of Zen for the great revelation that will figuratively push them off the roof into enlightenment?"

We sat in silence for a moment, and wondered how surreal elements could best be introduced into everyday life.

I looked out the window at the street outside. The downpour had been momentary. People had resumed their strolls on the sidewalk.

Without warning I found myself staring at a gigantic grinning red devil mask, goggling in through the window at me. Soccer-ball-sized yellow eyes bulged out of a blood-red goat's face; a giant cloth tongue lolled out from between carnivorous fangs; long dangerous horns swooped back from the head, and a bristly goatee spiked down from the narrow chin. The man wearing this mask must have been six and a half feet tall, and he was nearly naked, wearing only a loincloth, with his body painted all in red, and a long shiny tail in his hand, which he waved at me.

I waved back.

"That's pretty surreal," I said. "Well-timed, too."

"Thank you," she said.

The huge leering Satan danced away down the street, where I saw him meet up with a fair young maiden in a shepherdess costume, who took his arm as they pranced along the busy avenue.

"Yeah, that's rad!" I enthused. "People should do that all the time! Total street theater. I dig it."

"We have a lot of potential," Destiny said. "There is so much we could do. We want you to come up with new ideas. Do you want to play?"

She asked me this as if she were inviting me to a hand of cribbage, but the Game she was dealing me in to would change my life more than I ever dreamed when I said, "Yeah, all right, what do you want me to do?"

"We'll contact you with instructions," she told me.

I was becoming uncomfortably aware of my coffee-strained bladder. "Will you excuse me for a moment, please?" I asked.

"Certainly," said Destiny.

But when I came back from the bathroom, she was gone. Although I had not taken long, she had already paid for both our meals and disappeared.

I figured that was my cue to disappear, too.

As I was walking out the door of the Thai food restaurant, some kid who I'd never seen before, wearing a baseball cap and slouchy blue jeans, walked up to me and said, "Hey, Tim, wassup?" and then walked off.

*   *   *

Perhaps this is a good time, as we wait together in the ominous silence, for me to tell you something I haven't mentioned yet.

There are two versions of this story.

One is the version that you probably want to hear. It's the version that I usually I actually tell people, when they ask about this part of my life; which few people do, anymore.

Oh, I say all kinds of things in that version. It's a really great story.

I tell people that I dated Destiny for a few months, and that while I was dating her I got involved in some innocent activities like geocaching, or role playing games, creative anachronism, or the whole Burning Man scene. I tell a different version of my story depending on who I'm talking to; and I tell myself that it's *almost* true, because my involvement in the Reality Game may have been somewhat like some of these other activities in some ways, really.

There are many interesting details in the happy-ending version of my story: fascinating people who I met along the way, exciting women who I loved; oh, yeah, it's got acrobats, stiltwalkers, jugglers, musicians, dancers, you name it.

I tell people that I had a series of life-affirming adventures with perhaps some pagan or otherwise spiritual overtones, and that these experiences gave me a new appreciation for my own personal destiny, my individual role in an interconnected universe.

That's the version of the story I always tell people, because that's the story people want to hear: the inspirational, positive, hopeful story with a happy ending. People want to hear a story which tells them that all people are essentially good, when you get right down to it. People want to be told that all the answers may be found inside ourselves, if we just know how to look; and above all, people want to pretend that anyone really can succeed, if they just believe in themselves and try hard enough. That's what people want to be told; and sometimes, since that's what they want to hear, sometimes that's the version of this story that I tell them.

The main thread running through that more beautiful, more popular, more dishonest sibling of my true story, is the narrative of my enchanted romance with Destiny: a love which transported us into soft focus days of bliss together; a love which turned out to be tragically short-lived, in the end; but it's better to have loved and lost, as they say, and at least we broke up with no more than the most average of bad feelings; and then a few weeks later, I got into a completely unrelated car wreck with a hit and run driver.

I try not to mention that my apartment burned down on the same day.

You can believe that version of my story, if you want to. You can just imagine that all the rest of what I'm about to relate was just my own paranoid delusions. You can try to tell me that it was all in my head. You wouldn't be the first.

You can choose what you want to believe.

The Reality Game

The next day, I received a call from one of the Game Masters. He identified himself as my handler, and instructed me to be on the alert for future communications from him. My handler never told me his name, and I never found out how many other handlers the organization might have had.

By the time he called, I had definitely decided to join the Reality Game... and to try to forget about Destiny. I figured she was out of my league. It had seemed clear from our conversation that she was only interested in me as a potential recruit for her organization; not as a potential lover.

So that's why I was quite pleasantly surprised when Destiny actually did call me on my personal cell phone a couple days later. Bumbling over my words, I invited her over to my apartment; and my amorous hopes surged when she accepted! So I told her where I live, and she was only a few minutes late.

It was amazing. Destiny was actually there, at my place. This absolute dream of a girl was in my apartment, acting interested in all my shit, laughing and responding to my inane chatter. I couldn't believe my good fortune.

I never doubted for a moment that my fortune was in fact good.

I sat down really close to her and she didn't scoot back. Our knees were almost touching.

You don't know how befuddling it was for me to talk to this woman. I couldn't get used to it. I had rarely even seen a woman so beautiful, except on magazine covers, in advertisements, or maybe at a particular sort of adult dance club... Trying to sit across the table from her was so distracting that I was incapable of voicing reasonable suspicions about her identity, her motives, or her story.

Instead of asking such important questions, I began spouting the first thing that came to mind, doubtless revealing far too much personal information about myself in the process, information that could be used against me later.

Along with my whole entire life story, I revealed my real name, my real age, my real birthplace (with her innocent, "where are you from?"), and my high school mascot.

I even gave her my real date of birth. Sure, I did! First I told her my age, and then she said, "Really, what's your sign?" And I hate astrology, but I told her my damn sign anyway, and she said, "Really, that month?" And I said, "Yeah," and she said, "Me too! What day is your birthday?" And I told her, and she said her birthday was only a few days before or after mine, and wasn't that nice.

Nice, indeed. I probably even mentioned my actual mother's actual maiden name before I was done. What can I say? She was hot, and I was trying to impress her. Soon, she knew everything there was to know about me, and she'd only had to ask me a few simple questions, and to tell me some lies in exchange.

Next thing I knew, the subject and tone of the conversation had changed. No longer was it a personal conversation with intimate overtones: now she was talking about the Game Masters again.

In reply, I said I still couldn't figure out what their game was all about.

"Well, think of it like a chess game," she told me. "There are a large number of pawns who do things like you saw the people on the street doing earlier. They are street theater. They make appropriately timed entrances, sometimes deliver a prop or a line, and then they bugger off. Their interaction with the target is minimal. They are nearly scenery; but the combined effect of their actions provides a surrealistic situation for the target, thus magnifying the effect of whatever larger event has been scripted."

"So they're the pawns. Who are the back row pieces?"

"There is an elite group that plays a version of our Game against each other; again, like a game of chess."

"And what constitutes checkmate?"

"When you out-maneuver the other team to the point where they don't have any options. Look, it's not exactly like chess, that's just an analogy. It might be more like capture the flag, or something. No analogy is really accurate because it is unlike any game you have ever played. It is the Reality Game."

Just then my cell phone rang. I cursed, fumbled for the phone, silenced its ridiculous ringtone and put it down without looking to see who was calling, but Destiny said, "Go ahead, answer it."

"It's time," said the voice of my anonymous handler. He gave me an address. I wondered if he used a voice disguiser, while I wordlessly wrote down the location information. "Ten minutes," he concluded, and hung up.

"Shit," I said. "I knew they were going to call me about this eventually, but I didn't expect it to be right now. This sucks. I think I should just—"

"You should go," said Destiny. "I'll wait for you here. This is your first one, right? It won't take long. They always start you off easy."

I was very hopeful: so hopeful, in fact, that I foolishly believed her. "You'll wait here?"

"I'll be here when you get back," she promised.

I ran most of the way to the address I had been given. I had just arrived there when an expensive car pulled up beside me. The electric window in the back seat was smoothly lowered, and a large man in a dark suit wordlessly handed me a chicken. The car drove off before I even had time to stammer a protest. I wondered if I was the target of this bizarre incident, and not a player as I had been led to believe. Then my cell phone rang from a blocked caller ID. As I had been instructed, I was already wearing a hands-free headset for my wireless device.

"Walk down the street three buildings," my handler said. I did so. "Now, take a right, down the driveway."

I edged past a car parked there. I could see inside to a well-lit kitchen where a silhouetted figure was standing at the counter, doing something.

"Wait a moment," said the voice. My handler must be able to see me, I thought, and looked around, wondering where they were.

"Okay, on my mark," said my handler, "toss the chicken through the window, and then crouch down until I give you the all clear. Be very, very quiet."

I waited, hoping the chicken would not squawk, then wondering why it was not already squawking. It was pretty placid, for a chicken. Maybe it had had a long day; or maybe they had drugged it.

"Now!"

I tossed the chicken through the window and crouched down as fast as I could. There was a commotion inside, and someone said, "Who did that?" and I could hear them looking out the window directly above me, but they couldn't see me from this angle, pressed up against the wall as I was. They stayed there a frighteningly long time, then I could hear them move away, towards the front door, and the voice in my earpiece said, "Go now, quietly."

I ran as fast as I could. What was I doing, throwing chickens through people's windows? I sincerely hoped the chicken would be alright. I wondered what the point of the prank had been. A commentary on the target's courage, perhaps?

When I got back home, Destiny was no longer there. There was only a cheery note she had left in her place, written in a loopy, girly hand.

I tried calling her. There was no answer, and when it rang through to voicemail, it was not Destiny's voice, but a system message, informing me that no mailbox had been set up for this number.

I was young and foolish, and I did not change the locks to my apartment door.

Involved

I had several more assignments at the "pawn" level of the Reality Game organization. It was all creative anachronism stuff, like some of those Cacophony Society people do: bizarrely outfitted flash mobs and other completely harmless tomfoolery.

Once or twice I was asked to dress in costume and dance past a certain window at a certain time.

On several different occasions they told me to call out random names or words from some hidden location. For example, once I was instructed to station myself in a park, behind a tree, and when I received a text message signal, I was to cry out the name "Robert!" as loud as I could.

I didn't know who Robert might be. I imagined a variety of different scenarios. Most likely, Robert was the target of the prank. Perhaps the target, this "Robert," was unknowingly walking in the presence of a bugged operative of the Game Masters, who was secretly feeding the controller with information about the target's location. Perhaps the Game Masters were blackmailing the target. Perhaps "Robert" was not the target at all, but a name that held some special significance to the target. Perhaps Robert was the target's secret lover, or someone the target had murdered, or someone who had bribed the target, or who was threatening the target. The operative would steer the conversation to a certain topic when they reached a location in the park, and a team coordinator, listening to the bug, would send the signal at that time. Perhaps we were shouting his name to agitate the target, to exacerbate the target's sense of guilt and unease.

But I just knew I wasn't involved in that type of group. Criminals threaten people with guns; they don't call out names from behind trees. Our operation was involved in entertaining people, nothing more. I was certain. I told myself this, over and over.

I got the signal on my cell phone, but just as I was about to shout, "Robert!" someone on the far side of the small valley yelled it first. I yelled my "Robert!" in response and was surprised to hear two more people should "Robert!" from behind me. There were four of us! I had not been informed that I would be working as part of a team. The Game Masters were messing with my reality, too. I yelled "Robert!" again, and the others all shouted "Robert!" too, until we all started yipping and yapping and howling out "Robert!" the way a pack of coyotes will let out an excited flurry of yipping howls once they have surrounded their prey, just before they make a kill.

"Who the fuck is that?" yelled someone from the pathway that ran along the bottom of the little valley.

I turned and ran up the hill, crashing loudly through the bushes as I continued to yell, "Robert!" In the distance, I could hear the others doing the same. I never saw any of them; or the target, either. I never saw who Robert was, or whether he was alone, or if he was walking with Destiny.

After all this yelling for Robert, I was told my next operation would be a treasure hunt. I was to be a portion of the bizarre background for a certain target; but at the end of the treasure hunt, I would win a prize, according to my handler.

"Hey, can you put me in touch with Destiny?" I asked impulsively.

After a pause the man told me, "She is unavailable."

"How can I get ahold of her?" I blurted.

There was a pause. "She'll call you," the voice told me expressionlessly.

The line went dead.

*   *   *

The text message, when it came, was nothing more than an intersection and a time.

I went. The address was in the warehouse district. There was no one there. The streets and buildings were dark and deserted. I read the text message again. I was certain I was where I was meant to be, and that the time was upon me. Was I meant to find some clue in my general environment? I did not see any obvious sign or message. I could see no clue. There were no band flyers stapled to a light pole, no arrows drawn on the sidewalk, no balloons or paper plates. I checked all four corners. Finally, as I was returning to the corner where I started, I saw the message scrawled on the wall in three-foot high letters of fresh paint:

Meet us three blocks south.

You have got to be kidding me, I thought.

I walked the distance. A door opened on a car parked there in the dark and the shadows. "Come on in," said a voice.

I got into the back, and found myself sitting next to a man in an alien mask. The man in the front passenger seat had a giant bug head, and the driver was not wearing a mask, but had on an oversized chauffeur's hat that made it difficult for me to see his face.

"Welcome to the Reality Game," said the alien. "We're so honored that you want to play."

"We know you're just going to have a blast," said the bug.

"Great," I said. "What are we doing?"

"It's Christmas, and you're Santa Claus," said the alien, even though the evidence was against him on both counts.

"I'm sorry?" I said.

"*Des cadeaux*," said the bug-head.

"I give out gifts?"

"We're your jolly sleigh," said the alien.

"But I have no gifts to give," I objected.

"We'll get you some, at our next stop."

But when we got there, rather than a festive atmosphere, everyone seemed very tense. Some of them had guns, and one of them acted like he would have behaved aggressively towards me, because I was an outsider; which seemed odd, since I would have thought they would have first targeted my companions, who were wearing monster masks. But one of the other men held back the aggressive one, and I never really understood what the whole incident had been about.

There was only one gift, and it was very plain to behold: a mere cardboard box, unmarked, sealed in packing tape.

An old man handed it to me, and then my companion with the bug head took him aside for a huddle while the alien told me about the remainder of my mission. I was to make somebody's day by handing them the box, he said. It seemed odd, but simple enough. I asked the alien what was in the box, it seemed kind of heavy.

"Dreams," he said. "The box is full of dreams."

I must say, I felt somewhat suspicious at this point, but I was in a car with three of them, and that would make it hard to get away. I couldn't see myself jumping out a moving car just to escape. Even if I did try it, and I survived the roll, I would be stuck on foot in the middle of nowhere, and they would have a car. Playing out that scenario in my mind, it didn't end well.

So I delivered the cardboard box sealed in packing tape to an utterly unremarkable door on a completely normal street, and the person behind the door casually propped the box on its side and handed me a small brown paper bag.

The man with the alien mask took this bag from me when I returned. Opening it, he showed me the wads of money at the bottom. He retrieved a fistful of bills, and handed them to me.

"Merry Christmas," he said.

I took the money.

"But the best surprise is still to come," said the man with the bug head mask.

"It is?" I asked. I was thinking I had already enjoyed my fair share of surprises for one day.

"It is," averred the driver.

"It's true," said the alien. "The final clue of your treasure hunt will be waiting at your home."

When I returned to my apartment, it had been visited by a pot of gold. Gleaming, shining, fresh paint and burnished metal and molded plastic, there was a new TV, a new stereo, a new DVD player, and a new laptop computer. All my other stuff seemed to be there, stacked in a corner, and in the case of my old VCR, tossed casually into the trash.

I didn't even wonder if any of this stuff might be stolen. I could not allow myself to ask such questions. I only allowed myself to wonder if I might have to give it all back someday.

Blackmail

Well, after that, the next couple of pranks were more of the harmless stuff; but then one day I got a call, and my handler asked me to do something... wrong.

"You want me to do WHAT?" I asked in shock.

"You heard me," he replied.

"No," I said, "I didn't join up with this to hurt people."

"Oh, but brother," my handler cajoled, "just imagine how it brings the people peace of mind, to go through this and come out safe on the other side."

"This could mentally scar them for life," I protested reasonably.

"Oh, don't be such a little pussy," my handler snapped. "It won't do that. We've carefully preselected our targets. They'll be fine."

"I'm not going to do it," I said defiantly.

"Tim," said my handler in a warning tone, "you have less choice in this matter than you may imagine."

"What can you do to me?" I scoffed at his authority. "You can't make me do things I don't want to do."

"We could have the police at your apartment in ten minutes," said the voice on the phone. "They would find that your place is full of stolen goods. They would find your face on a surveillance tape near the times of the robberies when those goods were stolen.

"We have a photo," he continued, "of a convicted felon handing you something out a car window, and we have a photo of you making a drug delivery to a known member of an organized crime syndicate. We can even prove," he said slyly, "that you retained some of the cash from that narcotics transaction. Those bills are traceable, Tim. It can all be traced back to you."

I tried to remain calm. Don't panic, I told myself. Think. What is this group's *modus operandi*? Surprise, facilitated by illusion. What is the nature of an illusion? It is false.

"How do I know those guys are really criminals like you say they are?" I asked.

"Ask your heart," the anonymous voice said mockingly.

Without much confidence I said, "You're lying."

"Look in the top drawer of your desk."

I opened it up and saw a collage of images, images of my face and someone else's face. There were pictures of us alone, pictures of the two of us together, and then at the bottom, a newspaper clipping with the other guy's face and a headline announcing his conviction for activities related to organized crime. It looked like a real newspaper.

"Look it up online if you think the article is bogus or forged," growled my contact. "This guy is the real deal."

"I never even met him," I said.

"And yet we have photographic evidence of your association with him. Deny it all you like. If this goes to court, we can bring in experts who will testify that this photograph has not been doctored or altered in any way, and the judge and jury will believe the expert witness.

"So you see, we're not *asking* you if you want to continue your participation in our little Reality Game. We're *telling* you that if you don't follow instructions, the police will find out that your apartment is full of stolen property. The district attorney will learn that you have ties to organized crime, and the judge will never believe your extraordinarily unlikely story. You could even subpoena your own phone records to trace this call: the records will show that you were on a phone sex chat line. Your bank accounts will be frozen, your possessions will be auctioned off, and you will serve hard time; and after several years you'll get out with nothing. Is that what you want?"

I made no response. I wished I could find out who I was talking to, so I could track him down and pound his head in with a rock.

"Is that what you want, Tim?" the caller insisted. "I can have the cops there in minutes. Is that what you want?"

I let the silence hang for an ominously long time, but I realized that I didn't really have a choice in the matter.

"No," I finally breathed resignedly.

"Good choice," said my adversary. "Now, someone will be there in only a few minutes to deliver the essential supplies you will require for this mission."

My anonymous contact, when they arrived, gave me a dropper full of a clear liquid substance, and a photo of my target, and told me where I could find him.

The destination was a local bar, not far from my apartment. I had been there several times before; but this time was different.

I didn't know who my target was. All I had was a photograph and a location.

I watched him surreptitiously, there at the bar, while staking him out and awaiting an opportunity to complete my mission.   I even accidentally made eye contact with him at one point while I was watching him. He looked directly at me, his face expressionless, then looked away.

He seemed to be nobody special. He was just some guy.

He appeared to be about my age. In fact, he looked quite a bit like me, down to the stubbly facial hair. I imagined that he probably earned an un-spectacular wage at an uninteresting job, and spent his free time eating junk food and watching reruns on TV. I speculated that he most likely held disinterestedly to mainstream politics and noncommittal religious views.

I waited until he went off to the bathroom, and then I walked over to where he had been sitting. As I had been instructed to do, I opened the vial that had been given to me by my contact, and emptied its contents into his beer. Soon after he drank it down, he would be very surprised to feel the effects of the powerful hallucinogen.

I returned to my own table just in time to see my target walking past it. Was my table on his way back from the bathroom, or had he taken a detour? I couldn't allow myself to be paranoid. I finished my drink and departed.

Some twenty minutes later, I started tripping balls

My head spinning uncontrollably, I realized that my target must have been assigned to dose me, just as I had been assigned to dose him. The Game Masters were playing us against each other.

That's when things got weird.

Out of Favor

Well, it's obvious how it all ends, isn't it.

I don't even know for sure what I did to earn their wrath. Did I somehow inadvertently share a deadly secret? Prove incompetent? Wink at the wrong woman? Had I asked too many questions? Or perhaps the problem was that I had remained as obstinately rebellious as ever; or, on the other hand, perhaps I was really just another disposable operative who outlived his usefulness. Or was I ironically too useful, perhaps? Did I challenge their authority by refusing an order? Was it because I had not wanted to pour psychological chemical agents into the beverage of an unsuspecting citizen? I still can't even imagine anything I might have possibly done that could have truly been a threat to them. But based on results, I'm certain that I must have incurred their wrath in some way.

Whatever it was, they couldn't just let me go. They had to torment me first. (Practice for the new recruits, you see.) And when the Game Masters want to torment you... well, you think you're going insane.

I had been an insider, so I knew their methods, and still I couldn't even be certain that they were targeting me, or which incidents they were behind, and which incidents were coincidental happenstance. Is that guy looking at me? Is that car following me? Did I hear something? Was it just the wind, or the house shifting, or the cat? Usually it was. But sometimes I would find that my things had been moved. Whenever I couldn't find something, I thought the invisible intruders were fucking with me again. Had I moved the items myself? No, I was certain this indicated that an intruder had been in my home. But when? Had they broken in while I was there? Did they return? Did they remain?

When I left the apartment and ventured outside, random strangers approached me and seemed to know everything about me: my name and employment history, who my friends are, and what my activities for the last few weeks have been.

At work, I opened one particular e-mail attachment, thinking it would contain new instructions from the Game Masters; but it turned out to be a computer virus that attacked my employer's entire network and wiped the customer database.

That's the day I was approached by an undercover detective; or at least, that's what he claimed to be, but I didn't believe him.

"We understand that you have become involved with a group of individuals who call themselves the Game Masters," he told me. "These people have represented their organization to you in a certain light, and you have begun to participate in their activities, believing it to be just good fun. It is my duty to warn you, Mr. O'Brien, that these individuals are not who they claim to be: that they are in fact very dangerous and highly skilled criminals. The purpose of their activities is other than what they represent it to be, and it would be highly prudent of you to discontinue your association with them immediately."

I should have said, "How do you know this?" Instead I only asked, "Why shouldn't I associate with whoever I choose?"

"They have established a pattern," he informed me. "They've done this several times; but they're good at it. They never leave behind any incriminating tracks, traces, or evidence that ties them to the incidents. They establish themselves on a trust relationship with an unsuspecting and gullible individual who will play the part of the patsy." I wasn't too pleased with this description of myself, but was not given a chance to interrupt. "They involve this patsy in their activities," he continued, "which gradually escalate and become more and more bizarre and frightening. As the deviousness of their pranks increases, the patsy's sense of proportion gradually fades, and that individual's sense of the rules of the real world gradually blur. As soon as the patsy is habituated to engaging in aberrant behavior and will perform acts of criminal mischief without consideration, the patsy is sacrificed.   Usually the patsy is assigned a task that is too blatant, too brazen, and is in fact no more than a diversionary tactic. Several individuals who were once like yourself associated with this particular group and are now serving hard time, yet none of them has ever been able to provide us with enough information to so much as get a court order for a phone tap. We suspect certain individuals of ties to the organization but can prove nothing. I urge you to discontinue your association with them." He paused, and looked at me for a moment, then, and said, "And if you insist on being involved in them, at least gather enough information to buy yourself a plea bargain."

I was not in a mental space conducive to forming verbal replies. I nodded. I wondered if he was working for the Reality Masters.

"Oh, and one more thing," he said. "The woman."

I looked at him blankly.

"She calls herself Destiny?" he prodded.

I was surprised, but managed to stay silent.

"Stay away," he instructed me.   "She's trouble."

"Trouble?" I managed to repeat.

He nodded gravely, then pointed to the ring finger on his left hand. "Trouble, as in, married," he said.

Then he nodded to me and walked away without another word, while I stood there on the empty roof of the empty building in the abandoned part of town, wondering what the hell was happening to my life.

*   *   *

A few days later, I was seated at the diner near my work, just trying to eat my lunch in peace and read a book, when she showed up, hovering above me, looking over my shoulder.

"Hello, Tim," she said.

I looked up and examined her face closely, to see if she was wearing some disguise; but this was no disguise.

I had never seen this woman before.

She was a complete stranger, good-looking enough in a way, but too old for me, and kind of frumpy-looking, if you'll pardon the expression.

"Let me guess," I said.

"I'm Destiny," she supplied, without letting me guess. "Nice to meet you again," she smiled, daring me to call out her lie.

"Yeah," I muttered noncommittally, and turned my attention back to my food.

"Aren't you going to invite me to sit down?" she asked petulantly.

"I don't even know who you are," I answered cagily.

"I just told you," she said, trying to sound friendly. "I'm Destiny."

"You're not Destiny," I scoffed.

"I am now."

"But, what? No. What happened to the other one?" I asked, looking around as if she might be hidden in the restaurant somewhere. No doubt she was in fact miles away by now.

"I'd like you to think of me as a new face for the same person."

"That doesn't work for me."

"Well, then, consider yourself lucky."

"Lucky? Why?"

"Most people only get one destiny, and they cannot escape it. Not many people get two Destinies. You did. You got to meet Destiny, twice. Make the most of it. Think of this as your second chance. Don't blow it."

"Sure," I said. "Listen, I'm just trying to finish my lunch in peace, and I'm reading this great book, it's near the end, there's somebody dressed as a succubus, and somebody else is tied to a rack, being tortured with a cat-o-nine-tails..."

But this Destiny wasn't listening to me. Instead, she interrupted with a poem.

"There once was a man from Nantucket," Destiny began reciting loudly, almost shouting.

"Oh, no," I said, looking around in embarrassment at the other diners nearby.

"Who had to carry it 'round in a bucket," she howled with added volume.

People were beginning to look. "A little quieter?" I suggested.

"It got left in a box," she went on even more loudly, and then paused. The entire room was silent for a brief moment, and all were staring at her. "At Thirteenth and Knox!" she concluded at a shout that could best be described as a holler.

"Wait, I thought," I said, certain that I had never heard this version of the limerick before, and trying to work out what it might signify.

"And if you don't get there soon, then you're *fuck*-ed!" she concluded with mirthful hilarity. It was clear that she was enjoying this. I wondered if the Destinies were low-level recruits like me, or if they had more authority within the Reality Game organization.

"It didn't even rhyme at the end," I complained.

She looked at me quizzically.

"The limerick," I said.

"Whatever," she said with dismissive scornfulness. "It was a slant rhyme. It's good enough for an unstable motherfucker like you!" Then she rudely flipped me the bird, and departed, gliding giggling out of the restaurant with a swish of her sassy ass.

"What the hell?" I asked in frustrated perplexity.

People were looking at me.

"Sorry," I said to them. "Um. Yeah. Bye," I added. I put some money down on the table, and hurriedly followed the fake Destiny out the door.

Naturally, she was nowhere to be seen.

Taking my cue from the dirty limerick she had recited, I ran on foot to the corner of 13th and Knox, just as fast as my legs could carry me; but when I got there, I saw nothing unusual. There was only a box. Wait. A cardboard box, sealed with packing tape, lying on the floor of an ancient ruin? *What does it have in its boxetses?* I was worried.

It was a collection of photos. They were photos of me. In each of the photos I was doing something that was difficult to identify. Taken alone, the images seemed random. Put all together, it began to seem clear that I had been involved in some very shady activities. It wasn't at all obvious what exactly those activities had been, but the look on my face in some of the photos made it obvious that I was trying to hide; and that in itself seemed to suggest my guilt.

*   *   *

After this, the frequency of strange greetings built up to an intolerable crescendo. I had been surprised before, by the sheer number of people who would be simultaneously engaged in a common, seemingly inconsequential objective as part of the Reality Game; but I had never before been the target. The effect was terrifying. No place was safe. The cashier at the burger joint, the bus driver, the homeless guy in a doorway, groups of children, sometimes people passing by who I never quite saw, they all knew my name. Now I understood the message conveyed to the target: *you are being watched. We know where you are, all the time.* The constant, inescapable reminders were maddening in their anonymity, for no one could have known better than I that the people who delivered these messages, these strangers publicly hailing me by my True Name, they merely thought they were playing a game, and some of them didn't even know that much. I could not send messages back through them, nor could I extract information from them; they were completely clueless, just as I had been.

As I rounded the corner, I passed two guys standing there arguing loudly about whether I was cool or not (definitely not, they eventually agreed). They ignored me as I walked past. *They probably don't even know that I'm the target*, I thought. *They'll probably figure it out later, but maybe not.* These particular two guys had developed highly sophisticated crystalline structures of arguments to support their positions, and were enumerating the facets, one by one: all this extrapolated from the little they knew about me, which was apparently little more than my full name, age, weight, and hair color. Quite the imaginations they had. I wondered how much of that exchange had been scripted. Probably not much. The two players had enthusiastically built upon their parts, devoted some energy to the conversation. It was still just a game to them.

It was no longer a game to me. It was a threat.

Framed

I didn't see the car that struck me until it was only a few feet away. It suddenly accelerated, and I didn't have time to get out of the way. Realizing that I really might die, I leapt for the sidewalk. The car struck me in the leg as it passed, and I crumpled to the concrete, crying out in pain.

When I returned to my apartment, it was on fire. I didn't even go in.

"Hey!" called a stranger's voice. I looked down the hallway, and didn't like the look of the men who were glaring at me. "There he is!" one of them shouted.

I didn't know who they were or what they wanted, and I wasn't in the mood to find out. I bolted through the stairway access door. Despite my aching leg, I climbed up the stairs. I figured they would assume I would head down, so I hoped to shake them off my trail by ascending in the opposite direction.

I climbed the stairs, holding the handrail. The stairwell was dimly lit. The walls were off-white, the railing cold rusty steel. The stairs themselves were of chipped concrete which echoed my footsteps up and down the floors, too loudly.

The whole place felt deeply sinister, like an old movie where bad guy scenes are filmed by tilted cameras. I imagined the door on the next landing opening as I approached and half a dozen men in black hockey masks ambushing me.

I reached the landing. I watched the door. It had not opened yet. I walked past it. My shadow crossed the door. My shadow was vague, hazy, blurry, indistinct, its borders indistinguishable in the off-white, dull grey dimness. It was as if the lights, casting an image of me, were calling into question my solidity, accusing me of having negotiable, dubious edges, symbolic of my inconstant way of life, the haziness of my shadow representing the unfocused sequence of random events I had allowed my existence to follow.

I glanced at the neon light behind its plastic grill. I was about to address the stairwell light, to ask it jauntily, out loud, whence it had found the nerve to question my moral and philosophical integrity. But just as I was about to speak, the light began to flicker. The coincidence just seemed too weird. I hurried on up the steps, a feeling of urgency mounting deep in my stomach.

My heart was beating hard, my breathing heavy.

The echoes of my footsteps bounced up and down the stairs. At least, I hoped the echoes were from my own feet. What was that? Was there someone below me? I stopped, but heard nothing. Little hairs all over my body prickled to attention. I looked over my shoulder, half expecting to see a man in an expensive suit watching me from the landing below. There was nobody there.

Adrenaline was coursing through my veins. Feeling foolish but also feeling genuinely frightened, I began to run up the stairs, taking two, sometimes three in a stride. The echoes grew chaotic. The lights on the next landing were flickering, too. My nerves were jangling when suddenly a door opened somewhere with a loud slam that I knew could not have been the echo of my footsteps. My startle reflex was so powerful I nearly lost my footing.

I turned, only to find myself facing the undercover cop who had warned me earlier.

"You thought you could get away with it, didn't you, Tim?" he accused.

"You've got to understand, please!" I cried. "I'm not trying to get away with anything!"

"Of course you aren't," he mocked scornfully. "That's why we have photos of you-"

"The photos are a set up! You know that! Remember? You warned me! I'm only told the place, I never know who I will be meeting me there, or why!"

"So you say. But perhaps your role in this organization goes much deeper. Perhaps you are the grand master, the chief conspirator, the Don, the crime lord, the head honcho, *el Presidente*, the puppeteer, the man in charge..." I was flabbergasted as he reeled off all these various terms. I thought he must be nearly done, but I was wrong, he kept going. "...the top strategist," he accused, "the Game Master above all other Game Masters."

"You must be kidding!" I protested. "I'm nobody, a mere peon, a pawn in a game I don't understand. I've been used by an organization I haven't really even seen, for purposes I cannot comprehend."

"And that," he answered cynically, "is exactly what the head of the organization would want us to believe."

*   *   *

When the police searched my apartment, they found that it was full of stolen property. The district attorney accused me of having ties to organized crime. I convinced my defense attorney to subpoena my own phone records, to try to identify the source of the calls from the Game Masters: but the records had been doctored to make it look like I had merely been talking on a phone sex chat line.

Months later, my case went to trial.

I was sitting next to my lawyer at the defense table with my hands bound in cold metal cuffs when the bailiff called court into session with an "All rise!"

Standing, I looked up expectantly at the judge who was to decide my fate. She walked in, looking very professional, not glancing in my direction. I shook my head in disbelief when I saw who it was.

The judge was Destiny.

It was the first Destiny, the one who had originally asked me to meet her for lunch.

I nudged my lawyer. "That's her," I said, and pointed.

"Yes," responded my lawyer. She didn't like me much, I could tell. "That's the judge," she told me in flat tones, as though stating the obvious to a moron.

"No," I insisted. "That's Destiny! She's the one who recruited me into the Reality Game!"

My lawyer favored me with a protracted eye roll. "Are you trying to get off with an insanity plea?" she asked with scornful contempt.

"No!" I said more loudly, attracting curious glances from around the courtroom as I gestured towards the judge. "That's really --"

But it didn't matter what I said.

My bank accounts were frozen, my possessions were auctioned off to pay for my legal bills, and I am currently serving hard time. In several years I'll be released into a world where I have nothing.

But I did get one final opportunity to speak with Destiny. She came to visit me in my prison cell after the sentencing hearing. I guess she just wanted to rub it in that she had won the Reality Game, and I had lost.

I was furious.

"You said I could make my life the way I wanted it to be," I accused. "You said I could choose!"

Destiny shrugged carelessly as she regarded my degraded circumstances. "But the thing is, I'm playing the game, too," she said matter-of-factly, "and I decided to make your life story turn out the way *I* wanted it to be."

"You said the outcome of the game was up to me!" I remonstrated, trying not to let my voice sound whiny but knowing that it did anyway.

Destiny gave me one of her expressionless glances for a moment, and then she said, "I lied."

I could think of nothing more to say.

After a pause, Destiny concluded, "Checkmate."

Then she turned, and walked away.

I don't expect to be released anytime in the next decade. The food here is terrible. I curse Destiny every day.

The Little Black Box

Chapter 1: Calling on Roger

It was a sunny Saturday in summertime, and I had the day off from work.

I knew I had to work in the morning on Sunday, the next day; but for this one glorious day, I was free.

I didn't have any real specific plans for the day. I thought maybe I would do some grocery shopping; and I was overdue for a trip down to the Laundromat to wash my clothes. With eight hours until the Laundromat closed, laundry was looking like a distinct possibility, if not a particularly inviting one. *I should do laundry*, I thought to myself; but I really didn't want to. All I really wanted to do was kick it, chill, take it easy, ride the groove train.

So I called Roger just before noon, and woke him up. He was pretty good-natured about it, though. "I must have been pretty out of it, pretty late last night," he said. We talked for a minute or two before he was like, "Why don't you just come over in a few?"

I didn't want to rush him or anything, so I kicked around the house for a little while. I listened to some music and bounced around to the tunes for a bit. I did a set of push-ups, and threw all my dirty clothes in a bag to prepare for the Laundromat later. I sliced some cheddar cheese onto a bagel, tossed it into the toaster oven, ate it with some lettuce and tomato, and washed it down with cold coffee while idly reading the personals ads in a free weekly paper from a month ago, which one of my roommates had left on the kitchen table.

I filled my Nalgene bottle with reconstituted orange juice, swilled some, tossed it into a backpack with the newspaper and my other essentials, and slid my shades up my nose as I locked the back door behind me.

Roger didn't live too far from me, and it was a pretty warm day in early summer, so I figured I'd just walk on over.

I walked rapidly, head up and rotating, feeling healthy and alert, and resigned to, if not completely fulfilled by, my meaningless, directionless life.

It's not that I was unhappy. I couldn't pinpoint any one specific complaint, the resolution of which would end all my troubles.

And yet, it was the slight incompleteness of my satisfaction which inexplicably filled my thoughts.

As I strode down the sunny sidewalk, past the grassy green lawns of my residential neighborhood, past the trees planted in the sidewalk at regular intervals, past the occasional flowerbed or man washing a car in a driveway, I catalogued my complaints: all the sources of my discontent in life.

I was dating an attractive young woman; and although I didn't feel particularly passionate about her, and really had no desire to marry her, we seemed to get along pretty well most of the time, and we had great sex, so I mean it was really all I needed in the relationship department. It was a bit much, in fact; for in truth part of me was dreading the thought of her calling anytime soon, for the last time I had seen her, we'd had a terrible row; and part of me was angry that she hadn't called, preferably with an apology; and part of me never wanted to see her again; while another part of me was clamoring for sexual intercourse at the soonest possible moment. Finally, the voice of Reason attempted to soothe my worries through rationalizations—all relationships have their ups and downs; this wasn't really that bad; you had to expect a disagreement or two whenever you got into any relationship with another person.

So, at least in principle, I had not been reading the personals ads that morning out of a desire to start a new relationship. Anyway, the paper was old, and I was not interested, I told myself: I just read the personals ads because they're funnier than the theater reviews. "Divorced White Christian female, 42, 5'5", 260 lbs., seeks affluent Christian male for serious relationship, marriage; my four children need a father figure who puts Jesus first. No alcohol, smoking or drugs." My mind rebelled against the idea that any man would hate himself so much that he would respond to an advertisement like that.

My living situation, on the other hand, was a source of tangible dissatisfaction. My roommates sometimes did things that annoyed me. One of them had left the same crusty pan and greasy dishes in the sink for fully two weeks, and they were still there. Every other day I moved them out of the way so I could use the sink, then put them back in the sink so I could use the counter. I had taken to hiding my own dishes, so there would be a clean plate and pan for me to use for my own meals. But, I told myself, all living partners have irritating habits, and at least Rick didn't throw huge parties every night with the stereo cranked until 5AM or whenever the coke started to wear off, like this guy Jonathan I'd lived with in college had done; and at least he didn't bang on the walls and scream, the way my old housemate Margaret used to do when she got laid, every god damned night. Still, I wasn't the guy's freakin' mother, he was old enough he shouldn't need somebody else to remind him to wash his own damn dishes. I didn't need that kind of bullshit at home; I had to put up with enough bullshit at work.

As with so many of my peers, if I were to name one aspect of my life which was the least satisfactory, it would of necessity be my work situation. I am an artist, but I have not been able to find steady work in my field. So I have to waste my time and drain my energy on menial service-related tasks, trying to be nice to people all day, trying not to react to the ones who intentionally insult me—and I had somehow landed a job in a field where this was a common occurrence. I was underpaid, my job itself was demeaning on several levels, my boss was entirely unsympathetic, and my chances for promotion were slim enough to squeeze through the hole in a zero. On many days I came home from work spiritually exhausted, lacking the motivation to even take my shoes off before I flopped out full-length on the couch. I'd hardly been practicing my art at all—I didn't often have time, and when I did find time, I didn't have the energy.

My mind was attempting to draw some sort of connecting line between any two of these complaints, to identify trends and sort out solutions; but all my theories, upon cross-examination, dissolved into a puff of logic, or perhaps short-term memory loss.

I passed the park, crossed a busy avenue, took a left at the grocery store, and walked another half-dozen blocks or so to Roger's house.

I passed by a man washing a car in the driveway next to Roger's house. I nodded to him, mumbled a "Howdy." He just stared at me, hard, as I walked past him, to the front door of Roger's house. I knew he was still watching, staring at me, cataloguing my features, as I knocked on the door.

I stared at the door for a while. It didn't open. It continued to not open.

When I felt absolutely certain that it really truly showed no sign of opening in the imminent future, I rang the doorbell, fighting an urge to turn around to look at the neighbor who was, I felt certain, still staring at me.

I watched the door, to see if ringing the doorbell would make it open farther than knocking on it had. No appreciable result was immediately apparent. I turned around. The neighbor acted like he was just washing his car, but he had clearly been watching me.

I rang the doorbell again, and finally heard slow heavy footsteps. The door opened, and Roger's face floated in the shadows within.

"Hey, Jeff," he said. "Sorry to keep you waiting. I kind of fell back asleep and I kept not being sure if there was somebody at the door or if I was still dreaming. Come on in."

Chapter 2: Philocydrine

So I was awarded the unparalleled privilege of watching Roger's morning routine, or at least of hanging out in his living room while he went through it. I pulled out the weekly paper from my backpack and sat on the grimy couch in the dim living room with blankets and heavy curtains drawn across all the windows, reading a very opinionated and in fact derisive article about some bureaucrat entrenched in the slimy politics of city government. The article went off at length, which was good, because it seemed like a long time before Roger came back into the living room. To his credit, when he did return, he brought me a cup of coffee, and this pleased me. He put a CD in the stereo, set the volume a couple touches too loud, and settled in a chair across from me. I sipped my coffee as he lit a cigarette.

He tried to offer an explanation for being so late in getting out of bed. "I was up real late last night, man. Wow, I just totally lost track of time, you know what I mean?"

"It happens to the best of us," I replied.

"This one probably wouldn't have ended so late if it hadn't started so late."

"Sounds like quite a night."

"It was, it was, I can't even tell you." He sipped his coffee, bobbed his head to the music. I thought about my pile of dirty laundry, the one that I was neglecting as I sat here in Roger's dark living room, feeling somewhat bored.

Perhaps he sensed this, or maybe it was the lyrics of whatever song was playing, for he said, "Oh yeah, that reminds me." He got up and left the room, returning with a wooden box with an engraved top, which he unlocked.

I checked the curtains, to make sure they were fully drawn.

Roger's wares were pre-weighed and bagged. He let you pick the ones you wanted. I probably thought longer about this than the matter's consideration truly necessitated, but it's often entertaining to consider all the possibilities. Plus Roger kept distracting me by passing me fatties. By the time I had selected a couple and handed him the cash, I was feeling pretty well distracted.

I guzzled the last of the coffee in my cup, gone cold from sitting. Roger was just kind of staring at a spot on the wall. Conscious of the lull in conversation, I cast about for a topic worthy of discussion, and landed on Roger's mysterious allusion to his late night the previous evening. I thought perhaps a woman had been involved, so I asked him about the previous evening's entertainments, in a general sort of way.

"Oh, that's a long story," he replied with a spark of eager interest, as though he was hoping I would press him for details. With only a little encouragement from me, Roger continued:

"Well, you know, back when I was studying chemistry in college, I didn't merely learn enough material to pass the class like all the pre-meds; I also stayed up late learning how all the different chemicals combined together and split each other apart, conducting my own experiments; and I took a lot of Psychology classes, too, almost enough to get a double minor, but I didn't take a couple of the core requirements for a minor, because I wasn't sufficiently interested in Freud's penis complex.

"My interest," he continued, "was in the physiology of the brain, the chemistry of the neural pathways, how pheromones and hormones and synapses dictate what we perceive and how we feel and behave. I can't tell you how much time I spent in the library, in college, reading everything I could get my hands on that would reveal the secrets of the brain's chemistry. I used to go out behind the library, smoke a spliff, then just devour scientific periodicals and draw diagrams of chemical bonds and chains until 3AM, 4AM, whenever I decided to head home for my three hours of sleep. Sometimes I just slept in the library, when they kept it open all night. Sometimes I snorted lines off my desk to help me stay awake. I was crazy back then. I didn't always get great grades, but I learned a lot.

"My senior year, I got an article published in a nationwide chemistry journal, about the chemical structures of serotonin, dopamine, and a variety of the MAO inhibitors they use as anti-depressants, as well as such analgesic compounds as Lysurgic Acid Diethylamide-25, and its naturally occurring counterparts, mescaline and psilocybin. My article only mentioned the hallucinogens in passing, really; it was just kind of a sideline tangent off my thesis, but it was a sideline tangent into which I've invested a lot of thought and research in the years since then. I could spend a lot of time telling you how caffeine and tetra-hydra-cannabinol combine with naturally occurring chemicals in your brain to alter your mood and mental function. But right now that's not as important as the experiments I've been doing.

"I once postulated the possibility of the perfect drug. The idea was to have a maximum of mood alteration without loss of motor coordination; to psychedelicize perception without disagreeable physical side effects; and to provide a really far-out experience without risk of overdose, insanity, or addiction. For years I've tried to figure out how this could be possible.

"Then while I was working on a totally unrelated side project in graduate school, about photosynthesis, in fact, I noticed a minor similarity between certain chemicals that all plants produce, and certain important chemicals that are found in the human brain. It was about patterning, more than the compounds involved in the structure, but it was a moment of recognition and inspiration. 'If I could just snip out this chain right here,' I thought, 'rearrange the structure of the covalent bonds, then reinsert that modified chain back into the sequence, well, I bet I could sell it on the street for big bucks.'

"Unfortunately, the link in the chain that I was targeting proved to be the very least reactive. It took me a long time to figure out how to break it without altering the whole chain.

"I guess I shouldn't bore you with the details. In the end, I finally figured out a solution that turned out to be far simpler than what I had imagined would be necessary. In a couple of hours I turned an assortment of cheap, easily obtained, perfectly legal and non-toxic chemicals into a sticky, smelly mess on my stove; and a couple hours after that, I had refined a brownish powder which was, by my calculations, 0.25% pure..."

He rattled off a chemical name I couldn't really digest, it sounded like tripto-hydra-tetra-diethyl-bromil-floro-carbo-deoxy-polymethylcarbonate, or something; it may have contained several additional syllables, and it may have omitted some or all of the ones I just mentioned; chemistry was never my area of expertise.

"I usually just call it Philocydrine," he continued, "because a major ingredient in the first batch was a Philodendron plant."

"Okay," I said, "Philocydrine, I can say that."

"So that was, what, six, eight months ago? I've refined the process since then, and I've been conducting experiments on Herman, my rat, who wasn't offered an option regarding his participation in this study; and on Lucille, my roommate's cat, who voluntarily and in fact without my consent ate a much larger amount than I ever would have given her. Damn cat ate it out of a pan in the kitchen while I was out having a smoke."

"How did she act?"

"You know, it had pretty much the same effect on both animals: it hardly phased them. They were a little hyperactive for a while, then they ate some food and drank some water, and then they just kind of hung out for a couple hours, and eventually they fell asleep, and when they woke up they acted fine. Neither of them behaved in the disoriented, drunken manner which one typically associates with the consumption of pharmaceuticals."

"So, are you telling me that this wonder-drug of yours doesn't do anything more than a cup of coffee? What's the point of all the hours with the sticky, smelly mess in your kitchen, when you could just make a cup of coffee for the same thing?"

"Patience, young warrior. You have not yet heard all there is to tell. What I established with my animal experimentation is that Philocydrene is non-toxic. No vomiting, dizziness, peeing blood or dying."

"I don't know if the FDA would let you mass-produce it for human consumption on the basis of such a study," I objected, attempting to mimic Roger's scholarly manner of elocution.

"No, of course not," he said, busy at work with yet another fatty. He looked at me and grinned. "But it was good enough for me."

I laughed. "Okay, and what have been the results of your clinical trials using human subjects?"

"I first tested it four weeks ago. I took a quarter of one gram, in the morning of a day off from work. In order to scientifically study the effects of philocydrene itself, I refrained from consumption of other substances."

He lit the fatty.

"You're keeping me in suspense," I said. "What did it do?"

He blew out a thick cloud of smoke and handed me the jay. "Big fat nothing," he said. "I was totally unimpressed. As far as I could tell, I could have just drank a cup of coffee and swallowed an Aspirin, and I probably would have gotten more out of it."

"Bummer," I said, coughing.

"Yeah," he said, "that's what I thought. But I went back over all my chemical diagrams very thoroughly, and I couldn't find any holes in my theory."

"But it didn't do anything to the rat," I pointed out.

"It didn't *seem* to do anything to the rat, from the perspective of an outside observer. It is impossible to know exactly what the rat experienced."

"Okay," I said, "so what did you have to do to make it good?"

"It is good," he said, "I just hadn't taken enough of it. I did another test: I quadrupled Herman's dosage to 4 grams. The rat acted slightly more berserk at the beginning, and after a couple hours he acted a little sedated – his reaction times were a little slow. Still, he exhibited neither stagger nor stupor. I played with him, so he wouldn't go to sleep quite as soon; and also so I could properly observe his behavior. He just acted like a rat, except he acted like he had time to think about things a bit before deciding what to do.

"So a week after my first self-experiment, I quadrupled my own dosage: I took precisely one-fourth of the amount I had just given to Herman, who is obviously much smaller than I am. At one gram, I found a mild but distinct psychotropic effect, similar to about half a gram of mushrooms."

"Right on," I commented.

"And, well, I've been adjusting the dosage since then. I try to leave a week between each trial so I won't build up a tolerance, but last night I came home drunk and got a little too excited and drank down a big pot of Philocydrene tea with chamomile for flavoring; and that's when things really started happening."

"Oh yeah?" I asked. "What kinds of things?"

"Oh, you know," he said, "the usual: breathing furniture, melting walls, flowing carpets, vivid colors and vaguely transparent overlays of intricate patterns that expand when you watch them."

"Now you're talking," I said.

"It was more than that, though," he said slowly. "It really made me think. It was designed to simultaneously stimulate as many different parts of the brain at once as possible. Memory, linguistics, perception, analysis: pretty much the whole cerebral cortex. It is probably too much for the user to process, which is why it does not increase function. If for example I tried to take the SAT while I was on it, some of my thoughts would be pretty distracting, and I would be unlikely to score highly. That said, it sure seems to speed things up in there," he said, knocking on his own skull.

My own brain did not feel sped up at the moment. "Huh," was all I could think of to say.

He grinned at me again. "That's right," he said.

But a question was forming itself in my brain, against my volition. It was not the question which I asked next. "Are you going to do it again today?" I asked, which should have seemed ridiculous, since he had previously told me that he waited a week between "experiments," except that he was acting a bit like he was on it right now.

"I might," he said; then, guessing at the question that I had not asked, "You want to try it?"

Chapter 3: A Beginner's Dose

Roger brewed up two batches of special Philocydrine infused chamomile tea: one with a "beginner's dose" for me, one with a larger "just did it twelve hours ago" dose for himself. When both were ready he handed me a huge mug and we toasted to sunny afternoons. We sat on his front steps to drink it. It wasn't as horrible as I had expected: more like a lawn-clipping smoothie than the moldy manure milkshake I had imagined. Roger smoked cigarettes and I watched his neighbor, who was, incredibly, still washing his spotless car, and watching us at the same time. Not that we were doing anything interesting.

"Is your neighbor always this neurotic?" I asked Roger in a voice inflected to carry no farther than his ears.

"Who?" said Roger. "Him? Oh, yeah, I guess so. I don't know. He hasn't been very friendly since I threw a party six months ago and he called the police over at 3AM to ask us to turn down the stereo, only it wasn't a stereo, it was a live band." Roger laughed.

"I see," I said. "I guess I could see where he might object, maybe."

"Yeah, but whatever, you know, we haven't done it again, so I'm trying to let all that go the way of the past; I'm just doing what I can."

"That's all there is," I agreed.

"Uh-huh. Hey, I'm all out of smokes and I could maybe get some beer, too. You mind if we take a walk down to the store?"

"Not a bit," I said, "but what about these?" indicating our half-empty mugs of tea.

"We'll just take 'em with us," he said. "You got that backpack? We'll put the empties in it."

"It's inside." So I got my bag, and we set off.

I wondered if the Philocydrene tea would make me vomit.

We walked the first block in silence. I guzzled the rest of my lukewarm tea. There was a bitter brownish sediment at the bottom of the cup.

"Should I swill this shit at the bottom?" I asked. I tried to swirl it a little, but it was too thick.

"Nah," said Roger, "well, there shouldn't be too much."

I didn't want to argue, at first, but I looked again at the bitter mud in my mug and decided that this would be an appropriate occasion for the shit-flinging jocularity which characterizes so many of my interactions.

"No," I said, "now that you mention it, this isn't really a lot of mud. I mean, if this mud were at the bottom of a river, I'd hardly notice it. Only difference is, if it was on the bottom of a river, I wouldn't have so much of it in my mouth already."

"Quit being such a pussy," he retorted with a chuckle. "It's little more than the barest dusting."

"You didn't even look dude! Seriously, did you put a shovelful from your garden in my mug or what? I mean, I think I read a report somewhere that the Army Corps of Engineers has already scheduled the construction of a bridge from one rim of this mug to the other, but there's so much mud down there, they're afraid their machines will get stuck." It was an insipid joke, and I knew it, but I was feeling light-headed, like my brain had turned into a pigeon, and it was trying to fly out of my skull.

"You," said Roger, "are full of shit. How do half a dozen grains of sand constitute a thick mud?"

"Half a dozen my ass!" I cried. "Look at this shit!" And I thrust the mug in his face.

He stopped walking and pushed my arm back. "Whoah there, watch the face," he said, looking at me. But I was still holding the mug out, so he peered inside. "That's," he said, "no, wait."

And without further ado he drained his own mug, and looked inside. "Yeah!" he said triumphantly, and then looked at mine again, and didn't say anything for a while.

"Yours has more than mine, doesn't it?" I asked. "You must feel like you've been draining a swamp!"

"Shee-it," Roger said quietly.

"What?" I asked, suddenly not feeling quite so jocular. I looked inside his mug. There was, without a doubt, considerably more sediment in mine. I laughed nervously, and said, "So I got yours, huh?"

He shook his head, then thumped it with his fist a couple times. "God damn," he said, "I musta been fuckin' stoned!"

"So, but it will be all right, right? Because this is still less than you give the rat, right?"

But Roger just shook his head again. Then he said in a low voice, "That's a lot more than what I give the rat. I've been building up a tolerance, you see. I just did some last night! And I had decided to do myself real good this time around. So I was going to take a rather hefty dose. And then like a fucking moron I went and gave it to you, instead! Jesus Christ!"

I didn't know how to reply to this. "You're kidding, right?" I said at last.

"Sorry, man," he said. "I'm sure you'll be all right, but it might be kind of intense for a while. But you're a pretty mellow guy, I'm sure you'll do fine. I'll hang out with you to make sure everything goes OK. Just think happy thoughts."

I wasn't thinking happy thoughts. I was thinking of me, dead of an overdose, the first casualty of this brand-new experimental drug; or perhaps lying in a brain-dead coma for the rest of my life. I was thinking of Jimi Hendrix and Janis Joplin.

Chapter 4: Running Away from Shadows

We were walking down a residential street on the way to the grocery store when something moved in the bushes of someone's carefully landscaped suburban yard across the street.

I have walked past enough shrubberies in my lifetime that I don't go getting paranoid about little rustles in broad daylight. Plenty of birds and neighborhood cats, as well as the occasional raccoon or possum, hide out in the leaves, and sometimes startle a bit when you walk past. I knew this, just as I knew you have to look out for doggy "landmines" when you walk in the grass.

But another part of my brain was arguing with this rationalization, and in support of this argument it was supplying me with repeated and unrequested instant playbacks of the movement I had just seen. It had not been a bird, or a cat, or even a dog; nor had it been a raccoon, or a possum, or even a badger. What had been strange about this movement was that I hadn't so much heard it as seen it, and I hadn't so much seen it as sensed it; for what I had half-seen, half sensed, was not so much a preexisting entity shifting its position, so much as a possibility passing along a probability continuum. It had seemed as though the shadows had drawn together, bunched up and taken a solid form. Most disconcerting was the impression that the shadow form had seemed to be watching me.

"Hey, Roger," I said.

"Huh?" he replied with uncharacteristic eloquence.

"Did you see that?" I asked, trying to keep my voice low.

"Whassat?"

"Something, uh, something moved," I managed by way of explanation.

"Yeah," he said, "lotsa things are gonna start moving, pretty soon here." He kind of chuckled, in his Roger way, but it wasn't very comforting. I hoped that the whole experience wouldn't turn into some paranoid nightmare where demons crawled out of the walls and my eye sockets turned into dead holes in my face.

Despite the sunlight, my skin prickled into goosebumps, and a cold, icy fist gripped my intestines and squeezed. The sound of a light breeze seemed to intensify the moment, as though it were the herald of some approaching dignitary, blowing a horn blast to announce the arrival of a new and special moment in our lives.

I was still feeling like the shadow was following me, which shouldn't have been so weird if you think about it; I mean, everyone and everything is followed by a shadow at all times; and in fact in this era of artificial lights, sometimes it is not even particularly disconcerting to have six shadows at once, like some magical god from India.

The difference was, this shadow did not appear to be connected to me, and more importantly, you have to understand, the shadows I'm generally accustomed to don't usually give me the impression that they are watching me.

We had to be getting close to the store by now, I told myself.

I had walked down this street countless times, but somehow, at that time, the distances involved seemed farther, and the houses we were walking past looked totally unfamiliar. Maybe I had just never really noticed them before... or maybe each individual blade of grass on their lawns had never waved at me before, while they were dancing some kind of dance, la la la, blades of grass dancing in the sun, somewhere between a waltz and a rumba.

I should probably mention that Roger, true to form, talked nonstop the whole way to the store; although I can't remember a word he said. I think it had something to do with a unique sexual encounter, as reported by "a friend" of his, but for some reason, I wasn't really paying attention. I think I was distracted by the way the leaves were spinning on the trees and shrubs, and the bright bands of color which curled around each other into intricate patterns in the sidewalk.

After some time, though, as we were crossing a street, he must have noticed that I hadn't said anything for a while, and he asked me, "How ya feelin', man?"

"I, uh," I said, and laughed, trying hard not to feel nervous about the shadowy figure which was lurking in the shrubbery, all the shrubbery; its vaporous form materialized under every bush, where it watched us pass, then moved on to the next shade. "I'm sort of going several directions at the same time," I managed to finish. By the time I had pronounced this brief sentence, the elf-lights in the grass had already shifted to a deeper color than they had been when I began speaking.

"Yeah!" Roger responded enthusiastically. "Up, down, and sideways. I know exactly what you mean." We rounded a corner. "And here we are."

I looked at the grocery store. It glared back at me. It was a gargantuan, concrete monstrosity, a monolithic testament to consumerism, splattered with signs and posters, glowing with neon, even in the daylight, like a radioactive firecracker frozen in mid-detonation.

The store was on the corner of a major intersection, and there was much rumbling and growling from the engines going past. The cars in the parking lot were none too quiet, either, and in fact shortly after we began walking across the field of asphalt, I felt compelled to run, in an attempt to avoid being horribly mangled by a demonic mother of three in her bright, shiny, almost-new urban death machine.

Cars rumbled past me. I feared for the safety of my toes. One impolite individual was so impudent as to blare his screaming horn at little pedestrian me for trying to cross his path there in the parking lot.

At last we were across the parking lot and were nearing the yawning jaws of shopping central. Part of me was responsibly recalling that I was in need of some groceries, but as I stepped into the fluorescent lights my senses were overwhelmed by the swarm of insectile shoppers, the clicking and shuffling noises of the checkout cashiers and the strange, foreign-sounding murmur of maggots that was the combined babble of a myriad of voices.

"Hey Roger," I called out as he rushed off into the madness. I don't think he heard me; he neither broke stride nor turned his head. I hesitated, then ran up and tapped his shoulder. "Hey dude," I said, "I, uh, I don't really need anything from the store right now. I think I'm gonna wait outside."

He looked at me as if I was a total stranger, then seemed to relax and said, "Okay." He seemed to examine my face, and then said, "You all right, man?"

"Yeah!" I almost shouted with nervous energy, then in a more reasonable tone continued, "I just don't want to be in here right now, is all."

"All right," said Roger, "you want to wait outside? I'm just getting' a few things, shouldn't take long, I'll see ya in a few." And with that he was sucked into the vortex of shelving and lighting and crowds of people and signs that said things like, "Best Value!"

The mundane experience of setting foot inside a grocery store had so unnerved me that I had temporarily forgotten about the shadow that was following me... until I had re-negotiated the moving obstacle course of death in the parking lot and returned to the relative safety of the sidewalk beside the building.

Once I reached the sidewalk, I was sort of at a loss as to what exactly I was going to do with myself until Roger got done in the store. I didn't want to just stand there, looking like an idiot, someone might wonder what I was doing and think I was some kind of criminal loiterer and call the police or something. I supposed I could sit down and lean against the wall, keep low and hope I was not noticed... but the fact is, I hate to not be engaged in some activity. But then what else was I going to do? I didn't want to go too far, because I didn't want to miss Roger when he came out of the store. I was uncertain, undecided, unsure, confusing myself with all the possibilities, and I looked down at the ground... and there it was.

I jumped in alarm. I shrieked in fear, although my throat was constricted and the sound did not carry. I startled so violently that my arm jerked out to one side and I got a burning crick in my neck.

"Oh, fuck," I said, concerning my neck; but then when I looked back down, the Shadow was still there, a little off to one side, kind of shifting, kind of spidery, and to tell you the truth, really scary. I looked at it, and it looked back at me.

A quick walk around the block suddenly seemed like a really good idea.

Of course I knew it could keep up, but I didn't want it to get the idea that I was going to be friendly with it.

I walked fast.

As I walked, part of me thought to wonder what the hell it was.

And part of me was afraid I already knew.

As I fled from the Sinister Spider Shadow, I traveled into a place where time stopped. I left the street; I left suburbia and all the traffic and noise; and suddenly, in a burning flash of revelation, I learned something about my life. I discovered how sweet my pointless existence had truly been, when suddenly I found myself separated from that existence.

I gazed about myself, dumbfounded. Where a moment before I had been surrounded by the noise and traffic of the city, I now found myself in the midst of a mysterious wood, with no sound but the rustling of leaves and the calling of birds. I was quite alone, and appeared to be traveling down a small trail which twisted through the undergrowth ahead, until it wandered around a corner and disappeared into the trees.

The bonus seemed to be that, for the moment, I could not see the Shadow which had been pursuing me. The major drawback seemed to be that I was hopelessly lost, and I had clearly left my home neighborhood far behind.

There was, apparently, nothing I could do but follow the path through the woods; so, trepidatiously, I set one foot before the other and made my way into the unknown.

Chapter 5: A Poetry Reading in the Forest

I had hardly followed the path round the little corner through the trees and the bushes when my conception of my total solitude was shattered of a sudden: voices I heard, there! I jumped from the trail, hoping to conceal myself in the shrubs which grew alongside. I crouched down and strained my ears, wondering what sort of people might be about; but the voices drew not nigh; they were words spoken by one unseen, or so it seemed; and as there was naught about the voice which seemed threatening, I crept forward in hopes of glimpsing the speaker.

I peeked out from behind a fern. There, just beyond the path, hardly a stone's throw away, stood a young man, about my age, standing with his back towards me. I was uncertain as to whom his oratory was directed, or if perhaps he was, as it seemed, alone, and possibly mad. I was struck at once by his outlandish dress; it was colorfully rustic, in the manner of one who might dress up for a costume show, pretending to have lived hundreds of years ago, in a land far across the sea. Indeed, he resembled nothing so much as a play-actor, an impression he did nothing to lessen with his next words, which were these:

"Come, then, we shall have a poetry reading. This one is called, The Voices in the Forest."

He cleared his throat, and recited this poem:

The Voices in the Forest

There are voices in the forest,
    in the shadow, in the shade,
And they've whispered to each other
    ever since the world was made.

The wind cries in the treetops
    as they rustle up above
And it sings its sad lament
    searching for its absent love.

The birds, as through the air they wheel,
    cry out their lonely cry,
"We could suffer an eternity
    but still we'd have to die."

Still the singing of the insects
    fills the silence in my ears;
Yet *their* cry is but a lust for blood,
    and their death brings me no tears.

But down there in the shadows
      where the mold and mushrooms grow
I sometimes hear a whispering,
      perhaps from far below.

It speaks to me of time long gone
      and days still yet to come;
It sings to me of summers long
      and magic spells undone.

I've gazed into the shadows,
      but no speaker there I find.
I fear the voices whisp'ring
      are but voices in my mind.

I gaze to the lonely treetops
      and my longing eyes implore
But they speak to me no secret,
      they'll be silent evermore;

Save when the wind is blowing
      or a bug may chance to sing,
Or the winding wood may hear the call
      of songbirds on the wing.

My lonely heart calls them all dear
      but my soul, it longs for rest.
Tho all these whispers call me near
      I still love yours the best.

He took a bow, and I wondered if perhaps his audience was the very Shadow that had followed me, or if mayhap he had told his poem to the very voices in his mind to which he had made rhyming reference.

Thinking these thoughts, I was surprised to hear someone clapping; there was a laugh, too, and a fair voice, praising the young man's words. It was a lady's voice, melodious and sweet, a voice with such beauty it bespoke the beauty of the speaker. Hearing her speak, I desired to see her speak, for I was captivated, and wished to know my captor's identity.

It caused me some trouble, scratches on my hands and face, dirt on my clothes, leaves in my hair, for I could not immediately ascertain the whereabouts of My Lady, and though I wished to gaze upon her, I wished my own presence to remain unknown; so I crept stealthily through the undergrowth to the detriment of my clothes but to my own eventual enlightenment, for finally it was my fortune to learn from whence that shimmering voice had emanated; and what I saw there was better even than I had hoped: there, on a wooden seat, nestled under an overhanging bower of branches, sat the Princess of my Heart.

Obviously it would be ridiculous to pretend that I had always loved her, for I had never lain eyes upon her up to this very moment. Yet as I allowed my eyes to roam over her fair features, I felt that it would never again be possible for me to love any other. It was not only her voice, which was a silvery musical syrup sticking to my eardrums. Nay, and it was not merely her face neither, though a fairer one had never adorned a mortal. There was more to her beauty than the shapeliness of her figure, striking as it was. And I was certainly astonished by more than her fashion of dress, although if I had not already been so completely taken aback by the rest of her, those clothes would certainly have made me wonder.

She was attired as a May Queen, or a princess of old. Her hair flowed about her shoulders, adorned in ribbons, its ends teasing her breasts. She was clad in white, in a gown elegant in its simplicity, with lace ruffles at the sleeve cuffs, and a bright sash about her waist. I longed for her to move, that I might remember for the rest of my days the movements of her body; yet I longed for her to lie just so, that I might recall in future nights the vision of her beauty.

Neither stand nor recline did she, but sat up straight, and began a recitation apparently meant to be her contribution to the poetry reading.

The Lusty Joy of Springtime

The sun shone bright,
    the wind was fair,
The screeching of the crows
    echoed in the air.

The grass was soft,
  the grass was long,
She lay upon the grass and thought
  that she could do no wrong.

The lusty joy of springtime
  was burning in her blood;
Her fertile mind was blossoming,
  her life had changed for good.

She jumped then, and did somersaults:
  upon her head she turned,
And she stood there on her hands
  till the sun her ass did burn.

She ran naked through the forest,
  for her body it was bare,
'Til she came unto a grassy dell:
  and then she saw him there.

Upon his back in the grass he lay,
  and he had it in his hand;
Full naked in the light of day
  he stroked his manly gland.

She stared in curiosity
  to see this task performed.
She never in her life had seen
  a young man thus adorned.

She gazed upon the young man's face
        and the curls in his hair.
She thought that she had never seen
        a boy who was so fair.

And running then unto his side
        and aiding in his task,
She told this boy that she would do
        whatever he did ask.

Quite startled was this boy to find
        that he was not alone.
He gazed into the maiden's face
        embarrassed of his bone:

"One moment thought I, you were she!
        But now I see, alas!
For my heart I have sworn," said he,
        "I love another lass."

Whispered "Calm thyself" warmed ear,
        "forget that other lass.
For you are there, and I am here:
        a pretty piece of ass."

And looking up the young man saw
        that what she said was true.
"All that you could ask," he said,
        "is what I'll give to you."

And drew they then to an embrace,
       soft skin pressed against skin.
She said, "Please let me kiss your face
       before you slide it in."

Their kiss it was electric,
       both bodies felt a shock.
His hand felt all her body,
       Her hand groped for his cock.

Then up and down his neck kissed she
       and moaned he in her ear.
He squeezed then both her nipples
       and kissed away her fears.

He fingered her and she was wet,
       she looked him in the eye.
Then placed he there his hard hard cock
       and slid it in; she said, "Oh, my!"

The feeling it was magical,
       the joy it was intense,
For she was hot and slippery
       and he felt so immense.

And moved they there together
       and they shuddered, it was such
Fulfillment in each tiny move,
       ecstasy, each touch.

Long tarried they upon the grass
    full in the light of day.
He satisfied her till she begged:
    Yes, she was a good lay.

And long they lay there gazing
    into each other's eyes.
She said, "This lasts forever,
    a moment never dies."

The love they had was nameless
    and perfect in its throes.
Now part of it goes with him
    everywhere he goes.

I was shocked to hear such ribald lewdness issue forth from such a pretty face. She delivered the poem without a blush, quite as if she'd been reciting a pastoral piece about the frolicking of lambs, or maybe one about the color of the flowers in her back yard.

I found, too, that I was standing at attention, so to speak, and for a brief moment actually considered engaging in the activity performed by her tale's hero.

My thoughts were interrupted by the fully clothed young man in the glade before me, who seemed to be deep in conversation with someone much shorter than himself. He turned, and I saw that he was speaking to none other than the shadow which had been pursuing me.

The shadow, I saw now, had only appeared spidery before because it had not yet completed the rather complex process of consolidating itself into a solid entity. It now stood, squat, pokey, fell and evil-looking, about three feet high, with warts and scales and hair on its splotchy skin. It was some kind of goblin, or gremlin, or small troll, like a gargoyle, or a miniature demon. Its major characteristics were all pointy: pointy ears, pointy tail, lots of sharp pointy teeth, long pointy grasping talons, and a prickly habit of bouncing back and forth from one foot to the other and shouting. It was currently engaged in such a ridiculous performance, with its shouting and its hopping, that I didn't know if I wanted to laugh, or kick it.

I had been forgetting that I was, in fact, supposed to be in concealment, hiding in the bushes. I had begun to imagine that I was watching these characters on a movie screen; but at that point it ceased to matter, for the young man turned now towards me, and looking through the shrubbery behind which I was hiding and into my eyes, he spoke these words:

"You don't have to hide in the bushes, you know. I mean, we're doing all this for your benefit anyway, so obviously if you think the view is better from back there you're welcome to it; but if you'd like to step out in he open, you're welcome to do that as well."

Feeling very foolish, but halfheartedly hoping to be introduced to the pretty girl, I stepped out from behind the bushes and onto a little lawn. She didn't seem to notice me, but the demon-shadow sure did; he was pointing at me and jumping up and down and, well, squawking at me. I'm afraid there is no better word than "squawking" to describe the awful sound that the beast made at this time, and although the word carries with it the majority of the necessary imagery, it still lacks something, the ugly surreality of the beast and its beastly noises.

"This is Tory," said the young man. "He is Bad Thoughts."

Suddenly the little demon's face filled my whole field of vision, and I had a close inspection of how much dental work he needed as he hissed at me, "I am the Keeper of the Little Black Box!"

Having said this, he apparently seemed satisfied with his task for the present moment and without further ado marched across the grass and disappeared into the bushes.

"Black Box?" I asked my strange companion in some bewilderment. "What the hell was he talking about?"

"He won't say," the stranger replied. "In fact, he's just told you more about it than he's told anybody else in 25 years."

"Twenty-five years!" I exclaimed, surprised. "That's a while."

"A lifetime," my companion agreed.

"I wonder what his deal is."

"You could follow him and see," my companion suggested.

Now, why I should have done this is not at all clear to me now, as I think back on it. The fact is, I didn't want to have anything more to do with the little goblin named Tory. I could have never seen him again for the rest of my life and felt perfectly happy. What I really wanted was an introduction to that girl over there, whatever her name was. I saw her check me out. I should have just walked up to her at that point and said, "Hi," but I didn't know what was going to come after that, and I thought she was probably the girlfriend of the guy standing next to me, or something; so in a fit of shyness I ran down the trail in the woods, chasing Tory the troll.

Chapter 6: The Little Black Box

I went around a corner and down a small hillock. The tree branches must have grown closer together here, for the light was dimmer, and the air felt cold, too; clammy, as thought there were a marsh or swamp nearby.

There sat Tory upon an old tree-stump. In his hand was a perfectly nondescript boxy black thing.

"This is the Black Box!" he screeched. "I am the Keeper of the Little Black Box!"

"Yeah, yeah, you already said that," I told him, hoping he wouldn't bite, and hoping I wouldn't get infected, if he did. "So what? Why should I care about this thing you have here?"

He hid the box behind his back and looked at me with a gleam in his eye. "It's yours," he said.

"It is?" I said. "Okay then, give it to me."

He shrieked, "You don't even know what it is!"

"Well of course not," I said, "I haven't looked at it yet. If it's really mine, you should hand it to me, although I'm not sure I even want it."

He threw the box into a marshy ditch behind some nearby bushes. "Get it yourself," he said.

So I trudged out into the muck and slime that had maybe once been some runoff rainwater, before it stagnated in the mud for a couple of months. My foot slipped, and I got smelly muck all over my hand when I caught my balance, and my mind was filled with malicious thoughts about the little demon when suddenly I bumped against something big: a flat black wall. Touching it made my bones freeze.

I looked up at something that was the same basic shape and dull blackness as the Little Black Box, but it had been magnified somehow: it had grown to the size of a small house. I looked at it and panicked so hard I nearly passed out. I tried to run away and look small and talk my way out of it, all at the same time, and ended up doing nothing, just staring at the Black Box. It seemed to be staring back at me. Annoying little Tory had been an angel in comparison to this empty Thing. Tory was horrible, but in a ridiculously cartoonish sort of way. The horror that filled me as I beheld The Black Box was a nameless dread, an abject terror; it was as if everything I had ever hated or feared was there, locked inside it. Standing there, confronting it, I wanted to scream, but could not find my voice; or rather, I know where my voice was, I just couldn't make it work.

"You are nothing," The Box spoke as letters in my brain. "You are nothing."

"There, you see?" said Tory triumphantly from behind me. "That's why you need me to keep it for you."

"I don't want it," I said.

"Oh, but you can never get away from it," Tory said.

"Well, I've never seen it before!"

"That doesn't mean it wasn't there."

"And I've never seen you before, either," I pointed out.

"Isn't it nicer to have to deal with some silly little thing that you can laugh at, than it is to have to come into direct contact with the cesspool of all the mental sludge that's been dredged into The Little Black Box?"

I turned from The Box and looked at its ogreish Keeper. I didn't feel like laughing now.

"I liked the poetry readings in the meadow better," I said.

"Typical," said Tory, but I decided I didn't want to spend any more time with him. I slipped while going back up the slope out of the ditch, getting even muddier than before. I could hear him laughing at me as I tried to wipe the muck off my hands.

I made my way back to the footpath, but it didn't look the same as before. It was less a path now, and more of a trail; in fact it was HARDLY a trail; and to make matters worse it seemed to have more trails leading off it, in every direction, so that I wasn't at all sure which one I should take to get back to the sunny meadow with the beautiful girl.

I set off down one, thinking it was roughly the right direction, but the woods I walked past didn't look familiar. I told myself that I'd been in a hurry, when I had come this way last, but I kept walking and kept walking and couldn't find the little hillock I'd run down before. Perplexed, I stopped; but the bushes rustled, and I was afraid little goblin-faced Tory would be catching up with me at any moment, so I took off running, and came around a corner with a big old rotten stump, and found that I was back where I had started when I'd taken that path.

"Well, that was a bloody waste of time," I said, and set off down a different trail.

This one immediately started going up, but I soon realized that instead of climbing the little hillock back to the meadow, I was in fact on my way up a much larger hill. Instead of turning back, I determined to forge ahead in the hopes of viewing the surrounding countryside, and if I couldn't see the Poetry Glade from the top of the hill, perhaps I could figure out how to get back to my home in the suburbs. Even if Roger got two cases of beer and a whole carton of cigarettes, and enough chips and salsa for a week, he was probably done with his shopping by now.

But the trail I was following, after inclining steeply for several hundred yards, leveled off in a dense patch of wood, affording me no view at all. I hoped maybe the trail would wrap around the hill and slowly wind its way up to the top, but after another couple hundred yards I could see where I was headed—across a wooded ridge to another hill off in the distance. That was farther than I was prepared to go without first knowing where I was and which direction I really wanted to head. I looked up the hillside to my left. It was fairly steep, but there wasn't too much undergrowth. "What the hell," I said, and began clambering up the hillside.

I bent nearly double, to keep my center of gravity low. I grasped at roots and rocks and felt that I was making pretty good time up the slope, walking ape-style. But I wasn't really looking where I was going until I reached the top of a particularly steep scramble and came face to face with a vertical rock wall.

I looked down below, where I had come from. The loose rocks had slipped away under my feet as I came up; I could just picture myself riding an avalanche all the way back down to the bottom. On either side of the point where I stood, the ground dropped off even more sharply.

Trying to assess the situation, I moved towards the rock face. A stone slipped under my foot, and I lost my balance. I pitched forward, clawed frantically at the rock wall before me, and barely held my position, swaying, with my head leaning over a yawning abyss, with a perfect view of a stone that I'd kicked loose, as it fell, and fell, and fell, and fell, before it hit the rocks at the bottom, so far away I couldn't hear it above the pounding of the falls.

"Ah, shit," I said.

Feeling now that my position was perilously precarious, I decided my only option at this point was to keep going up, and hope I could find a better way down from there.

Grasping at the edges of a boulder, I hauled myself up onto it, steadying myself against the rock behind it. The face was a columnar basalt, with many chips and broken places, so that I could almost envision a trail of stairs, from my current position, sideways and upwards, to the ledge above. The face was not entirely as vertical as it had first appeared, and as long as I didn't look down, the sense of vertigo wasn't too bad, and I could just imagine that I was climbing a very peculiar flight of stairs.

I reached the ledge without incident, and was starting to feel some pride in my freestyle rock-climbing. How my rope-bound, course-snotty climbing friends would yell if they saw me now!

Then I tried to figure out where I was going from here, and began to wish that I had a rope, and was wearing a harness, and a helmet, and that someone was belaying me from below; for the rock face was quite steep, here, and hand holds not as plentiful. I could see another stairstep pattern, a little up and to my right, but it was well out of my reach, and in order to get there I could see that I would have to traverse a practically smooth face, using little more than the friction of my fingertips to keep me from sliding to my death.

I started upwards, found a hand hold, and another. With some difficulty I repeated this process, and looking over, saw that I was now about level with the staircase of broken rock that I was trying to reach.

Now to cross the smooth face.

I sidled up to it and though I could see a foothold on the far side. Would my leg stretch that far? I eased myself over, pulled up with my fingertips as I moved my right foot out over nothingness, and put my left foot where my right had been. My right, meanwhile, had found a temporary place to stand, but I was left in a very awkward position, with my body stretched out diagonally. I attempted to stand up straight, but found that I had no hand holds in this new position. At this moment my right foot's foothold turned out to be not a rock but just a clump of dirt which crumbled beneath my weight. I pushed off with my left foot as I started sliding straight down the smooth face, and with that push managed to grab with my hand the same bit of crumbly dirt that had recently betrayed my foot.

It held, for now.

I cast about until I felt another hand hold, and tried to pull myself up with it. As I did so, a rock bounced off my fingers, and it hurt so bad I nearly let go.

"Ow," I said.

From somewhere up above me I could hear someone snickering. I risked a glance. The crown of the hill was only a man's length above me, and there sitting on it was the little goblin, saliva dripping from his fangs as he laughed. Tory reached about him, looking for another stone to throw at me.

"Damn you, Tory," I said, "I swear, if you throw another rock at me, when I get up to the top I'm gonna throw you off."

But Tory just laughed louder, and then wandered out of my field of vision.

Between luck and stupidity I managed to scramble to the final set of stairsteps that I had seen from below, which I now used as hand holds. I was nearly within reach of the top of my climb when Tory re-entered my field of vision, holding a rock nearly as large as himself.

"Tory, you little-" I began, but he just laughed, and dropped the rock on my head. Or, at least, he tried to drop it on my head; but he missed, and the rock bounced off the wall above my head, scraped my shoulder on the way past, and clattered down the mountain below me.

Tory collapsed in a fanatical fit of maniacal laughter.

I found a hand hold, and then another, until at last I was reaching above the rim of the cliff I'd just climbed, and hauled myself over, panting.

Tory was laughing so hard there were tears coming from his eyes, and he was pounding the ground with his fists and feet.

I stooped over and picked him up.

He bit me.

"I told you," I said, and prepared to pitch him cliffwards.

"No!" he shrieked. "You can't! I am the Keeper of the Little Black Box!"

"Fuck you," I said, and threw him over the edge. "And your Little Black Box, too," I added as an afterthought, as he plummeted down to the rocks at the base of the cliff.

Feeling very relieved now, I looked about me. The hilltop where I stood was bald and grassy, with a large oak tree growing at its peak. This vantage afforded me an excellent view of the surrounding countryside. The drawback was, I'd never seen this countryside before. It was nowhere near my house in the suburbs, and in fact totally failed to resemble the world as I think of it in this day and age.

The world, as I know it, looks like a grid. The city streets lay out a pattern like graph paper. Flying by airplane and looking down at the countryside, it looks like a chessboard. Even forests have straight edges and square holes in them where the clear cuts have been logged. Land, as I have always known it, has borders with right angles.

But this land onto which I looked was not square, but lumpy. Ridge after ridge of forest I saw, as it must have been in the days of old, before the proliferation of Man. The wilderness stretched away unobstructed in all directions for as far as my eyes could see on this clear day.

I stood for several minutes, lost in thought. First I thought of the pure beauty of untainted, untamed Nature, the rugged openness of wild spaces. Then I began to wonder how I was going to get to work in the morning.

Slowly I turned about, taking a close examination of my surroundings. "Woods, woods, woods," I said to myself, seeing nothing but hills and valleys, with some rivers and a lot of trees, trees, trees.

Then at once I stopped, and stared: for there, between the outstretched arms of two ridges that fell away from the south face of the hillside, was a small town. I knew immediately that it was not my own town, however. For one thing, if nothing else had tipped me off, the architecture of the buildings was entirely unfamiliar to me. The buildings of this town were made of stone; not concrete, but actual stone; even the houses with thatched roofs. I could see, at the near edge of the town, nestled in tight in the bosom of the valley, stood a stone cathedral; and overlooking the town, at the point of a ridge off the hill opposite mine, was a castle- nay, a fortress, with turrets and fortified outer walls and everything.

If that wasn't enough of an indication that I was not looking at my home, the traffic through the town certainly was. Now, the town where I'm from has a lot of traffic, don't get me wrong – but the traffic to which I have become accustomed consists of motor vehicles: passenger sedans, Recreational Vehicles, economy cars, station wagons, motorcycles, luxury sedans driven by the nicest blind old retired people, and of course trucks, SUV's, tractor-trailers, and occasional police cars. Thus I really didn't know what to think when I realized that all the traffic in *this* town was drawn by horsepower in the most traditional sense: horses and mules and donkeys were down there on the streets, pulling buggies and carts full of people and vegetables and chickens in baskets. My mind froze. This didn't seem to have anything to do with Roger and his Philocydrene. I felt clear-headed and steady-handed, if a little dizzy from the height and my exertion. This was not a hallucination, I was certain; I was just quite simply and for no apparent reason hundreds of years and thousands of miles from where I was supposed to be.

Not two hours ago, my mind had been filled with all the little naggling annoyances that made my life less than perfect. Now as I stood on the hill looking at a life that was not recognizably mine, all I wanted was to get back to the world I knew. I could deal with my problems when I got there.

I turned all the way around again, but I was clearly not going to find a road that would take me to the suburbs. I was going to have to try to find a person, someone who could tell me where I was and how I got here.

The only obvious thing I could do was to head for the town. I didn't know how to get back to the beautiful poetry reading girl; I could see hundreds of small spaces between trees, from here, but I could not see her in any of them. Maybe she lived in the town, and maybe if I went there I would run into her again. No other options were evident at this juncture: I could either head for the little town, or I could wander around by myself in the forest out in the middle of nowhere. Granted, under other circumstances, this latter would have been an option I would have sought out for the sake of itself: the difference being, I would have remembered driving there, no matter how lost I got trying to get back to my car.

Without hope of a car, I took the only option which seemed to be logical. I took my bearings and tried to figure out approximately in which direction I would need to head in order to make my way to the distant village; and then I tried to find a path that would take me in that direction.

Naturally, there weren't any paths that headed in that direction. Indeed, the only paths I could find seemed to lead in precisely the opposite direction. I considered following one of these, in the hopes that it would wrap around the mountain and eventually head in the direction I wanted to travel; but the sky was cloudier here than it had been when I left my house to go to Roger's house, a long time ago, in another world. Looking down the hillside into the trees, I thought that once I was in the forest, it would be nearly impossible for me to be certain of the direction I was headed. The best plan, I decided without pausing to consider if there might be other alternatives, would be to start walking as nearly straight towards the town as I could, and I sighted along a sight line and made mental notes of large rocks and distinctive trees and such that would mark the right track.

And off I went! Down the hillside, almost at a run, ignoring the vines and thorns and thick underbrush that grabbed my feet and tried to trip me; ignored them, that is, until I found myself confronted by a thicket of densely grown shrubs – they were impassible, it would not be possible to proceed in a straight line. I took a mental note of a tree on a hill that I was supposed to head for, and went to the left, where the hillside fell away. The incline was steep, but regular for some time; then the hillside was cloven by the waist-deep, dry bed of a runoff creek, which I decided to follow, thinking that water finds the most direct route downwards, and that this ravine seemed to lead in the approximate direction that I wanted to travel.

Yes, my woodsmanship skills had apparently, for the most part, deserted me entirely, but it was not long before I saw my mistake. As I followed the ravine down, its course grew progressively steeper, while its sides were soon several times my own height, and so steep as to be virtually sheer. I scrambled down a couple of drops until I was well and truly committee to my course: and then suddenly there was no ground in front of me, just a piece of the sky which seemed to have somehow become confused with the ground. I looked at it for a while to try to determine how the sky had come to be there, in front of my feet, and sooner of later some part of my brain managed to put together the pieces of the puzzle, and my perspective resolved to reveal the it was I who was in the wrong place, high up on the side of a steep incline, looking at a life-ending drop in the face. I decided I didn't want to be there.

I turned around and started scrambling back up the steep ravine the way I had come in, but the dirt and rocks were loose, they slipped under my feet, and there wasn't much for my hands to grab onto. For a sickening instant I thought I would slide backwards and fall into the void.

"Yeah, this whole thing was really brilliant," said a voice in my head. "You get an opportunity to go for a beautiful nature hike and you end up looking into a canyon from the wrong side of the guard rail. You'll probably die here, and that's okay. In fact, good riddance. Anybody who's stupid enough to get into a predicament like this does not deserve to live long enough to pass on that 'dumb' gene to an unsuspecting new generation: there's no knowing WHAT that gene might get up to. May as well just..." and so on. I ignored the voice and pulled myself a little ways up the steep side of the ravine, using a little shrub as a handhold. The shrub gave way in my hand but I managed to crawl up onto a little ledge.

"Killing the vegetation, contributing to erosion," accused the voice in my head It was right, I knew, but I didn't want to DIE, so I was going to have to climb back up to the nearest ridge. I picked out a route, it looked steep but feasible, so I started scrambling. Dirt and mud on my clothes and face, dead leaves in my hair, these no longer presented themselves as issues requiring my attention. All that mattered was that I was moving up the hill.

"You've chosen your path poorly AGAIN," said the voice, although it seemed to be right, for in order to get to the next ledge, I was going to have to climb over a fallen log – a log which had, judging by appearances, already rolled quite some distance down the hill, and now was apparently delayed from continuing its plunge by nothing more than a minor snag. The log was caught on a thick bush which actually held one end of it suspended partway above the ground. From where I stood, though, the log was only high enough off the ground to guarantee its status as an obstacle, and to prevent any method of surmounting it, other than straddling it to climb over; which, my mental companion noted obtrusively, meant that I would be obliged to put some of my weight on it, which could make it start to roll; and if it didn't push me down backwards and break all my bones, it would pin me down and I wouldn't be able to move and I'd be stranded alone on a deserted hillside, far from any hope of rescue.

Up and over that log I climbed, and up to a ledge. From there I scrambled to another ledge, and so on, until finally I was hauling myself onto the ridge. I promised myself that for as long as possible I would follow ridges, not ravines.

I sat there for a minute catching my breath and wondering at the unfortunate turn of events. If any of several strategic rocks or twigs had slipped at just the wrong moment, my ravine excursion could well have proven fatal.

"It's karma trying to get you back," the voice had been saying in my head as I scrambled up the crumbling face of the ravine, "because if you die, well then it's no less than you deserve for being such a rat bastard. Why, just think of the way you treated that poor girl. She was so beautiful, and you were so selfish; you really showed her your true nature. Oh, and now you've got this other new chick wrapped around your finger, following you like she's tied on with string, but you're just using her."

"We have an understanding," I objected out loud, in a grunt. My voice sounded harsh in my ears, in the quiet of the forest. I suddenly realized how thirsty I was.

"You have an understanding," the voice yelled at me, "but do you think SHE understands? The fact is, and will remain, that she is more serious about this relationship than you are."

"All right, then maybe I should break up with her," I suggested.

"Oh, that would REALLY make her feel better," came the sarcastic rejoinder. "Show her what a generous soul you have."

I was not really sure what to say next but I wasn't given much time to think about it because the voice in my head continued. "You drag her along and try to act as though you like her, just long enough so that she puts out, and then you flush her like used toilet paper."

"I'm not like that!" I yelled at nobody, looking around in the hopes that nobody other than nobody had heard my outburst, sitting by myself there on the ridge. I noticed that I was in fact sitting on a path, possibly the very same path I had decided not to follow when I'd left the hilltop, only a few fateful minutes before.

"You sure would feel stupid if somebody came along and found you all muddy and tangled, arguing with yourself out in the forest," mocked the voice. "They'd cart you off to the loony bin, and right quick, too."

The voice in my head sounded familiar, so familiar that when it began speaking I had paid very little attention. However, it was starting to get on my nerves now, and I thought about it a little harder. It seemed that I had heard this voice for my whole life; it seemed to speak with my own voice, and until now I had never thought to question whether it was in fact just me thinking to myself. But today the voice was really annoying me and I began to suspect that something was transpiring which I had never suspected before. I stood up and looked around. Then I jumped back and nearly fell. A shiver ran down my spine, and all the hairs on my arms and scalp prickled.

The Black Box was there, ominously close, right behind where I'd been sitting. It was just a little bigger than a car, and I'd practically been leaning against it. Suddenly I felt very cold. Terror, dread, loathing, fear, hate and revulsion emanated from the Box and swirled behind my eyes, and I discovered that I was clenching my fists and my jaw.

"Get away from me!" I yelled at it. "I don't want you!"

"But I am a part of you," said the Little Black Box, grown huge and terrifying. "I'm the Voice of Discontent. You need me to motivate you. If you were happy with your life and pleased with yourself, you'd never get anything done."

"This is not the way," I said.

"Look," said the Box in my brain, "I know what I'm doing, and I'm not about to consider that your judgment is valid. You have done too many stupid things, too recently."

And with this, into my mind there sprang unbidden an image of myself that very day, stepping off the curb without paying attention as I was walking over to Roger's house, and nearly getting creamed by a car. Then I remembered a conversation I'd had the day before when I had said something entirely inappropriate and came off feeling and sounding very foolish. And to top it off I recalled the way a random stranger had recently said something very rude to me, a gas station clerk or something, and I had just silently accepted the insult and left, and couldn't think of a comeback until almost ten minutes later. Yes, I was utterly inept in quite a number of ways, especially my social skills, which perhaps explained my trouble sustaining satisfying relationships with women.

"Or maybe it's because you're incapable of loving anyone other than yourself," said a familiar voice in my head, a voice which sounded remarkably like my own.

My limbs were sagging. I felt burdened by excess gravity, filled with an overwhelming lethargy. I felt that I wanted to annul my perceptions, just go to sleep or something so I wouldn't have to keep thinking about all the mistakes I'd ever made.

"Why on earth did you..." the voice was accusing me, as I slowly lifted my head, forced my eyes to raise from the ground, squared my shoulders and fixed my gaze upon the Box. For some reason this was much more difficult than it should have been. My eyes kept looking above the Box, or off to one side; and when I tried to really focus on it, the Box itself seemed to waver and fluctuate from one side to the other, so that I never seemed to be able to look directly at it.

That is the nature of The Little Black Box, I explained it to myself. *It doesn't want you to be aware of its existence. Even after revealing itself to you, its intention is to recede back into your subconsciousness, where you will forget about it.*

At that time, however, I was all too aware of its existence, and I wanted it to go away. Approaching it was like trying to walk on the floor of a swimming pool: some invisible resistance tried to hold me back. I got mad and tried to kick the Box, but it was not only large, it was heavy and solid, and did not budge or seem to be affected in any way; I felt that I would be more likely to break my foot than to dent it. Trying to force myself to feel undaunted, I leaned my weight against it in hopes of toppling it, or scooting it off the path and over the side of the ridge. Even as I pushed against it with both hands, it seemed to be trying to escape from my field of vision.

And then suddenly there was a rent in my reality, and I fell through the tear: fell forward onto my hands and knees, and landed in blackness, as devoid of light as a pit beneath the earth.

Then the blackness opened up and I was falling, and as I fell I was assailed by images, memories, by fear and loathing. Everything I had ever regretted was flashing past me, things I had done that I hadn't thought about in years, things I had seen or that other people had said to me that I had long ago tried to forget. The collection was horrifying, and pathetic. My life, it implied, was a long-drawn scene of pointlessness and futility, stretching from the dismal and sordid past into the hopeless future. All my actions were pathetic, selfish, useless, misguided, secretly destructive. All my plans were empty excuses for the lack of a plan, and my life was directionless and meaningless. I fell and fell, plummeting into despondency, not caring where the plunge was taking me, until it occurred to me that I'd been falling for a suspiciously long time without hitting a bottom. I tried to stand up, and found that I could; the sensation of falling continued, but there was something floor-ish that provided resistance. It was something like a lightless, rapidly descending elevator. That was when I realized that I was actually inside the Little Black Box. I screamed and began pounding on the walls, trying to re-open the rent through which I had fallen.

"You can't get out," said the voice in my head, now booming and loud and seeming to come from all around me.

"There must be a way," I said, although I wasn't so sure.

"The Box is locked. No one has access to it."

"Tory did."

"Tory was just a porter, and occasionally a spokesman. He never had any real power."

"What are you?" I asked.

"I told you," the voice said, "but of course you never listen. I am the Little Black Box that lives in your mind. I am the Voice of Discontent. I am with you always."

"No!" I shouted. "There have been times, I have experienced moments when I was happy!"

"Never completely happy," the voice snarled. "Always in the back of your mind, your bad thoughts lurked."

"You're wrong!" I shouted. "They may not have lasted long, but I have lived moments when I was completely happy! There have been times when I have been able to put my fears aside!"

"Like what?" the voice challenged.

"There was the camping trip to the beach with my girlfriend last summer."

"You had a fight on the way there, it rained for four out of five days, and you were dreading going back to work at the end."

"Yes, but there was a moment in there, sandwiched between everything else, it may have only lasted for five minutes, but the sun came out and I lay on the sand next to the woman I loved, and everything was perfect and I had no regrets. I live for moments like that!" And with this declaration I plunged my head and arms into the wall of the Box. The wall gave way like gelatin, and coughing and sputtering, I dragged myself out.

I lay on the ground panting for a moment, then looked around. The Box seemed to have disappeared. Then I felt it: it was inside my head, right behind my eyeballs, filtering my impressions of the world.

"There is no escape from the voices in your head," said the voice in my head.

I started running as fast as I could, heedless of the sounds of maniacal laughter.

Chapter 7: The Dragon of Reason

After a time I was breathless and sweating, but at least the Little Black Box behind my eyes was, for the moment, not offering any new commentary.

Running downhill through the trees on that rough path was bad for my knees and ankles, but I kept at it for quite a while, until I was brought to a halt by a new dilemma: the path split into three distinctly separate trails, all heading in different directions. I could see none of the landmarks I'd noted from the top of the mountain. In fact, I couldn't remember what they had looked like. One was a tall pine tree with something funny about its top, I knew; but down here I could walk right underneath it and not know. There were some big rocks, too; but there were also many big rocks that did NOT indicate my chosen path, and anyway, all the damn big rock looked the same from a distance, and different when you got up close. Furthermore, to make matters more complicated, the sun was, as I had feared, completely hidden by trees and clouds; and of course the path I'd been following had twisted around a lot, so that I had absolutely no idea what direction I was facing.

I took a wild guess. It seemed likely that I'd turned left more than I had turned right, so I now turned down the path to my right.

I had not gone far when the trees began to thin somewhat, and as I came around a bend I saw that the path was about to take me through a broad meadow. I stopped to survey it, and smiled to myself without thinking. The meadow was carpeted with moss, and like a two-dimensional haze, a plane of small purple and blue flowers floated above the ground. Other than a large stone outcropping which stood midway across the field, it was remarkably flat. Just past the big boulders, the path went over a little wooden bridge, presumably to cross a creek which I couldn't see from here. I liked the looks of this part of my adventure: there was no way for me to end up dangling over a cliff as long as I stayed in flat places like this. I skipped, and almost ran, as I strode briskly into the purple-blue haze.

As I was approaching the rock outcropping, it occurred to me that now would be an excellent time to take my bearings relative to the sun. I stopped and craned my neck upwards, but no sun could I see; the sky was a uniform grey, with no break in the clouds or bright spot which would indicate hidden solar rays. Perplexed, I halted my forward momentum and turned in a full circle. The wide meadow in which I stood was semi-circular, though its borders were irregular. I was standing in the precise center of the field, or so it seemed, for in every direction patterns in the plants appeared as lines like rays extended outwards from the point where I stood. As I examined these patterns in the plants closely, I saw that they were not merely straight lines, they were in fact complex patterns; and as I watched the patterns it seemed as if they were shifting, revolving, rotating... I shook my head. I looked again. The patterns were still there, but different shapes now, infinitely complex, designs within designs. Most people would be in too much of a hurry to notice, I decided. I watched the patterns. They danced a slow, intricate dance. They seemed to be different colors now, or to have different colors mixed in with them; not just the blue and purple of the flowers against the greens of the moss and grass, but rows of red and yellow dots marched out and swirled around each other in mind-bogglingly complex formations, winding their dance around and folding in on themselves, only to burst open again in a joyously fractalific explosion of miniscule detail. I watched for some time, enraptured, totally forgetting that I was on my way somewhere.

At last, as I was wondering how such things could be possible, it occurred to me to wonder where I was. Maybe this was a special place, with a special type of vegetation. I looked around. The trees did seem to have a peculiar way of moving which could not be explained by a breeze. It was perplexing. I felt confused. It seemed as if all the world's energy converged on this place; it seemed as if all the events in my life had led up to this point in time, as if some grand revelation was about to shine out in all its glory, and the answers to the great questions, the very meaning of life, was imminent, and I was preparing to be immersed in the glory of enlightenment. I tilted my head back and held my arms outstretched, palms upward, waiting for the glorious answers to come unto me. And I stood like that and waited for a while, eyes closed in anticipation. And as I stood there my arms grew tired and I grew uncertain of what, precisely, I was waiting for. I opened my eyes. The sky was grey. I lowered my arms.

"Nice day, isn't it," a voice observed. I cringed, anticipating an attack from the hyper-critical Little Black Box in my head; but then it occurred to me that observations regarding the weather were not typical of the derogatory tone I had come to expect from the Box of Blackness.

Puzzled, I looked to my left, and to my right, but saw nothing other than the path through the meadow, stretching across it and disappearing into the trees on either side.

"Huh?" I said.

"I simply mentioned that it's a nice day," the voice repeated. "You seemed to be enjoying it."

I turned all the way around, and jumped backwards.

What I had earlier taken to be a large outcropping of stone had resolved itself into a large scaly creature, with a long neck, taloned feet and very sharp teeth. It was watching me.

"How you doin'?" it said casually. I found myself temporarily unable to reply. It did not seem particularly concerned with my ability or inability to speak. It went through a lengthy stretching process that apparently involved every muscle in its gargantuan body. It stretched out its long neck, then reached its forelegs as far forward as they would go. It appeared to stretch its front legs for some time. Then it walked its massive hind legs as far back as they would go, and stretched its monstrous, scaly back. It then stretched its hind legs. After this, it unfurled its wings, and spread them as wide as they would go, casting a broad shadow upon the ground, even in this dim light. I had to crouch down in order to avoid being knocked over by the massive span of its opened wings. I looked up in terror as it flapped them experimentally a few times, then folded them back against its sides. Last of all, it stretched out its long tail until it was totally straight, the spike at the end quivering with the effort.

"Ahh," it sighed at last, and collapsed upon the ground with a thud.

I was having quite a bit of difficulty coming to terms with the fact of its existence. Perhaps I should not have been so surprised, having recently thrown a goblin over a cliff with my own hands. My arm was still bruised and bleeding a bit from where Tory had bitten me. But the goblin had initially begun to materialize in the world of habit that I call reality, whereas this was something out of a children's story, a fairy tale, ancient mythology. I was looking at it, it had spoken to me, but I told myself it couldn't be real. It was... it was a...

"Dragon," I said to myself, out loud.

"Ah, yes, you're a perceptive one."

"I don't understand," I confessed.

"The Dragon of Reason, at your service," he introduced himself.

"... of Reason?" I echoed.

"We all have our specialties," he said. "I do my best to make some sense of the world around me, with the information that's available to me."

"You do."

"To the best of my ability."

"It just seems so unlikely. Did your mother name you the Dragon of Reason?"

"My name is who I am. Nobody had to tell me who I am. I just knew."

"You figured it out?"

"It stood to Reason."

"So, you believe that the rules of logic have a practical application in this world."

"To a certain extent."

"All right, then, why don't you tell me what the fuck is going on?"

"To what do you refer, precisely?" he asked, unperturbed by my rude manner. "There are always innumerable events transpiring simultaneously. Flowers grow, flowers die: the cycle of life. The wind blows, the clouds move: cause and effect. The sun rises and sets, the stars revolve and spin: astronomy and the relationships of physical objects to each other. Life, the universe, and in fact everything is in a constant state of change. Everything is always evolving, dissolving, and becoming—"

"Okay, okay," I interrupted, starting to feel dizzied by his words. "All mysticism aside, I'm just trying to figure out what's going on with me personally."

"What seems to be going on?" asked the reasonable dragon. "While they may sometimes be deceiving, appearances frequently provide valuable clues regarding actualities."

"I don't know where the fuck I am!" I exploded. "Nothing has made sense all day. I've been having conversations with people and creatures and even objects that couldn't possibly exist. I'm lost, and I'm tired, and I keep nearly dying in rock-climbing accidents."

"Have a fear of heights, do you?"

"No!" I shouted. "Well, only when I'm about to fall."

"I see."

"Well, where am I? Do you know?"

"Where do you think you are?"

"I think I landed inside a fucking fairy tale, is what I think. None of this could possibly be real. It's some kind of dream, but I don't know how to wake up."

"You are paying a visit to the World Inside," said the Dragon of Reason. "Do not let yourself be alarmed by the experience. If you can let yourself relax, you will do better at it."

"I will do better at what?"

"It's like a game," said the dragon. He was sitting up on his haunches now, smoking as he looked down at me. "As with most games, you have an objective here; the difference is, no one can tell you for certain what your objective is. You have to figure it out for yourself, and you have to be careful, because you could be wrong. There are no rules in this game. Well, I guess you could say there are the obvious laws of physics, and basic game protocol such as find and complete your objective without dying; but just as there are rules in the world you have come to think of as 'reality,' and under certain circumstances you permit yourself to break those rules, providing you're careful and don't get caught; similarly, the rules of the World Inside can be broken, if you know how."

"And if I just want to get back to the reality I'm familiar with, and maybe play this game of yours later, if I feel like it?"

"Well, first of all, it isn't MY game, it's just the way things are here. And as for your question, I'm afraid this isn't a game you can put down. Maybe getting back to reality is your prime objective, but it's unlikely. If it is, and you succeed, then you've won. But if you get back to reality without completing your true objective, the game won't be over, and some of the players could follow you back."

I laughed. "Well, I'll just have to try it and find out, then. How do I leave?"

"I don't know."

"Oh, come on, of course you do," I argued. "You're, like, my contact, right? You must know a way."

"There is always a portal, but it's never the same. You have to figure out where it will be, based on the context of the game, the clues that you get from the other players."

"Who are those other players, anyway? Who decides to let them play?"

"You do."

"I do!" I exclaimed. "You mean like I sat down and decided I wanted to play hide and seek with Tory the goblin and the Little Black Box from psychedelic hell? No way, man, you're crazy. I want nothing to do with them."

"You may not have realized it yet, but all the other players in this game represent something to you. None is completely figmentary; all are symbolic in some manner."

"And you are the Dragon of Reason," I said.

"I believe that's been established, yes."

"Why a dragon?"

"In Oriental mythology, dragons are symbolic of wisdom. In Western culture, the dragon is seen as a dangerous and unpredictable terrorist. Pure reasoning can be a dangerous and unpredictable path to wisdom. Therefore a dragon is an ideal choice for a philosopher. And furthermore," he looked down at himself, "The scales, the talons, the flying, the fire-breathing for God's sake: a dragon is raw power. Humans are enamored of power. The ability to reason well bestows power upon its possessor. Therefore a dragon is an ideal embodiment of Reason itself, and the Dragon of Reason is a player you'll want on your side. Since you asked."

I didn't say anything.

"You have more questions."

"What about the people I met earlier, reading poetry? Are they supposed to represent something, too?"

"The young man was a Hopeless Romantic," said the dragon. "And the young woman... if you don't know who she is, you should just ask her."

"Okay, okay. What do I do next?"

"You have to figure out your objectives."

"My objective is, I want to find a way home."

"I might caution you that what at first seems like a primary goal may in fact be merely a secondary aspect of achieving your true objective."

"Cut the crap, man. I just want to get out of here."

"Do you want me to help you, or not?"

I sighed. "Yes, please."

"Good. Now, think. What themes have emerged so far in this experience?"

"Uh, well, being lost in the woods has been a big one."

"Splendid. Now, what do you think that symbolizes?"

I looked at the dragon. He was stout, kind of portly for a dragon, as if he had an un-dragon-like penchant for cheeseburgers and potato chips.

"You want me to say," I accused him, "that being lost in the woods is, what, symbolic of my life and the directionless way I wander through it."

"You said it, not me."

"But that's what you think," I pursued.

A dragon is not a creature designed to shrug. Its shoulder blades are in the wrong place. Given this limitation, the Dragon of Reason's approximation of a shrug was an impressive performance. "It stands to reason," he explained.

"Sure, sure," I said. "Does that tell me how to get back?"

"No, it does not," said the dragon impatiently. "It's just a clue. Now, what other themes have emerged? Think about it. What has happened that has excited or upset you?"

"Well, I almost died. That upset me."

"But you did not die, and so long as you keep it that way, you'll be fine. What else? It will probably be something that involves other characters. Who was the first individual you met after the game started?"

"It was the poetry reading, wasn't it?"

He shook his scaly dragon head. He had lots of sharp teeth, and bony crests above his yellow, saurian eyes. Smoke trickled upwards from his nostrils. "You had a contact in the other world, your habitual reality, a contact which drew you into the game."

"No, I didn't," I said, and then stopped. "Oh, shit, you mean Tory the troll?"

"Precisely. How did Tory describe himself to you?"

"He said he was the keeper of the Little Black Box."

"And have you had contact with the Box of which he spoke?"

"Too much, already. It has insulted me and chased me, and I fell into it, and then somehow it fell into me, or something. I think it's in my head right now. I'd like to get it out, now that you mention it."

"Now, *that* is a worthy objective."

"Okay, so how do I do it?"

"Let's start with what you know about the Box itself."

"It told me that it is the Voice of Discontent. It follows me around. Sometimes it seems to be speaking inside my head."

"When you hear it speak inside your mind, does its voice sound familiar?"

"I guess it has kind of always been there," I mumbled.

"So the Little Black Box, as you perceive it in this world, is an externalized manifestation of a psychological phenomenon whose presence in your life has exhibited longstanding continuity?"

"Sure."

"I would venture the hypothesis," said the Dragon of Reason, "that most people possess some form of the Voice of Discontent. It may in fact be a biological aspect of the human mind. If that is the case, you would not be able to completely remove it and still be human. However, if its voice is overly distressing to you, if it speaks so loudly that you are paralyzed with fear and indecision, then clearly you will need to find a means of controlling it, to subvert it to your own purposes, to turn down the volume on that Little Black Box in your mind. Once you are able to do this, you will have more confidence in yourself; and true confidence is often self-reinforcing. When you feel confident, you act confident; when you act confident, other people are attracted to you, they take you seriously, they help you achieve your goals. Achieving your goals and being surrounded by people who are attracted to you makes you feel even more confident, and so on and so forth."

"You'll never be like that," the Little Black Box spoke up in my mind. "You're too pathetic."

"But how would I even get started?" I whined to the Dragon of Reason, cringing. "I don't know how to be any different from what I am!"

"You must have faith in yourself. You must learn to find the source of your inner power, and to channel it to your purposes."

"This is sounding suspiciously like some New-Age religious bullshit," I said accusingly.

"There is nothing so very 'New' about the concept of finding one's inner power," said the Dragon of Reason philosophically. "And there's not much truly religious about the idea that the Kingdom of Heaven is within."

"The Kingdom of Heaven?"

"Yes. Free your mind, and your ass will follow."

"Wait a minute..."

"No more waiting, no more minutes. If the Little Black Box is the voice of your discontent then I, the Dragon of Reason, am the voice of your logic and purpose. Like the Black Box itself, I am a manifestation of an aspect of your psyche. The time has come for us to do battle."

"But how would you battle the Little Black Box?"

The Dragon looked at me reasonably.

"I mean," I explained, "obviously you have the fire, and the talons, and the sharp teeth and the spiked tail; but if the Little Black Box is inside my head..."

"I shall call it out," the Dragon answered me. "First I shall conduct an incantation."

And with that, the Dragon of Reason began to weave an unreasonable magic spell. He drew symbols on the ground with his claws and with his tail, and he chanted strange words. As he chanted, the smoke from his nostrils formed into symbols which drifted through the air and shifted into other symbols before dissolving into shimmering almost-nothingness. His eyes blazed with purpose as the force of his spell took hold, and then he cried out in a powerful voice, "Voice of Discontent! You who call yourself the Little Black Box, come forth and answer my challenge!"

Suddenly the Little Black Box manifested itself there in the field, and there was nothing little about it; it was huge, the size of a city block, and it spoke with a voice of thunder that echoed from distant vales.

"Who are you to challenge me, useless dragon? Your puny spells can work no magic, your claws and fire cannot harm me, your words are dust."

"And yet you have answered my summons," the Dragon answered calmly.

"I came only to amuse myself by squashing you," the Black Box boomed.

"We shall see," said the dragon.

"Indeed," said the Black Box.

And then the two of them sat there, doing nothing for what seemed like a very long time. I wondered if I should just leave. The Dragon of Reason was a powerful ally, but the Little Black Box was a formidable foe; and if the two of them could hold each other in check, perhaps I could just leave them both behind and get on with my life.

The Black Box was still with me. "You will never leave me behind!" it screamed sinisterly.

"But maybe I can make you shut the fuck up once in a while!" I howled back at it in frustration. I reached down and began picking up whatever objects were at hand, and throwing them at the Black Box as it continued its silent standoff with the Dragon of Reason. I hurled stones, I cast sticks and branches, I tore up clods of dirt and clumps of moss, and finally I even plucked some of the little purple flowers that grew in the glen, and tossed them at the Little Black Box.

Its flawlessly smooth black surface bubbled and smoked where the flowers touched it. The flowers themselves vanished in a puff of acrid vapor, but they left behind a mark.

"Beauty!" called the Dragon of Reason. "Your sense of wonder at the beauty of the field; *that* is what can vanquish the unreasoning, all-encompassing hatred of the Little Black Box!"

And suddenly I knew this to be true. I plucked more of the blue and purple flowers and tossed them at the Black Box. Its surface writhed and smoked, and the Box itself grew smaller and smaller until at last it vanished.

"Did we win?" I asked the Dragon of Reason in surprise. "Is it gone?"

"It will never be gone forever," the Dragon of Reason answered, appearing tired from the effort of holding the Black Box at bay. "But now you know that your appreciation for beauty is capable of vanquishing your Voice of Discontent for a time."

It sounded somewhat corny; but I knew it to be true.

As I thought it over, the mountain meadow and the Dragon of Reason began to fade away.

Then I found myself lying on the ground beneath a tree in the local park, near the grocery store where I had left Roger, just a few blocks from my own house.

"Just look at yourself, rolling in the dirt," said a familiar voice which I now identified as the Little Black Box. "It suits you. Now you've probably missed the Laundromat, you've wasted the whole day and you'll be filthy for a week."

"What a beautiful day," I said out loud.

The Little Black Box made no reply.

The End